KV-636-163

SPECIAL MESSAGE TO READERS

THE FAR SIDE OF FEAR

With Stella, his secretary, away in San Francisco, laconic LA private eye Mike Faraday settles down for a quiet weekend. But then old man Frisby shows up unexpectedly, his life in danger, and Mike is plunged into a case of murder and mayhem. Frisby had found munitions stored in the warehouse where he worked, and three days later attempts on his life had started. Mike too is in danger as a huge, bald man tries to send him over a cliff, and then there is the intervention of the mysterious blonde, Myra.

Books by Basil Copper
in the Linford Mystery Library:

FLIP-SIDE
THE LONG REST
HANG LOOSE
BLOOD ON THE MOON
DARK ENTRY
SHOOT-OUT

BASIL COPPER

THE FAR SIDE OF FEAR

Complete and Unabridged

LINFORD
Leicester

First published in Great Britain in 1985

First Linford Edition
published 2005

British Library CIP Data

Copper Basil
The far side of fear.—Large print ed.—
Linford mystery library
1. Faraday, Mike (Fictitious character)—
Fiction 2. Private investigators—California
—Los Angeles—Fiction
3. Detective and mystery stories
4. Large type books
I. Title
823.9′14 [F]

ISBN 1–84395–769–8

Published by
F. A. Thorpe (Publishing)
Anstey, Leicestershire

Set by Words & Graphics Ltd.
Anstey, Leicestershire
Printed and bound in Great Britain by
T. J. International Ltd., Padstow, Cornwall

This book is printed on acid-free paper

1

I drew back the elastic band and let fly. The rolled pellet of silver foil zinged through the air and slammed into the glass partition. The bluebottle rose angrily, staggered into the air and then went out through the slats in the window-blinds. I felt better then, my aggression satisfied. You're a real killer, Faraday, I told myself.

It was Friday afternoon, one of the most deadly days of the week; Stella was out of town for a long week-end and I was holding the fort. I'd had a month of stake-out work in the spring rains, which is the deadliest time of the year in L.A. for that sort of assignment. But a private eye has to eat and it had kept the bills rolling on through.

I was missing Stella. And not only for the coffee, though she makes the best in the world. I stared over at her hooded typewriter and then glanced at my watch.

It wanted a minute to three-thirty.

The plastic fan went on abrading the edges of the silence. I ought to wait until four o'clock before I put the coffee on. That way it would help to get me through the afternoon. I wouldn't shut up shop and leave until five-thirty. Faraday Investigations were conscientious about things like that.

Despite the efforts of the fan there was a humid, cloying heat this afternoon. I stared over to where the sun shining through the plastic blind made barred stripes of black and gold on the floor. On the boulevard outside, in the smog and the gasoline fumes, the throb of the stalled traffic was rising to a nice crescendo.

I shifted my position in my swivel chair, conscious that there was a big patch of perspiration beginning to form in the small of my back. I lit a cigarette and feathered blue smoke toward the cracks in the ceiling. There was a faint footfall now, in the corridor outside the waiting room. I had the communicating door open, just in case someone had need of my services this afternoon. Not that it was likely. But one never knew.

And that way I'd know instantly someone tried the waiting room door. I put my spent match-stalk in the earthenware tray on my desk and listened to the footsteps. They passed the door and then went on. I relaxed again and glanced at the Examiner which was lying on my blotter. I'd read it from cover to cover but there might be something in the small ads which I'd missed in my anxiety to find out what had been going on in the L.A. basin.

The phone rang just then, with a jarring intrusion in the silence. When I came down from the ceiling I picked it up.

'Allday and Allday,' a woman's soft voice said.

I blinked but decided to humour her.

'And Allday and Everyday,' I said.

The woman at the other end made a heavy clicking noise with her tongue.

'This is no time for levity, young man.'

'Thanks for the compliment,' I said. 'But I'm not young. I'm thirty-three and full of no-coffee at the moment.'

She almost blew her top but she managed to hold on to the shreds of her temper.

'I want Allday and Allday, the lawyers,' she said.

'Try dialling the right number,' I said.

I put the phone down, conscious of the footsteps passing in the corridor again. It wasn't exactly gracious of me but that was the mood I was in. And it was the sort of afternoon it was, come to that. I grinned across at the large-scale map of L.A. we have tacked on the far wall. The phone rang again while I was doing that.

'Allday . . . ' the same voice began.

I sighed.

'Night just fell,' I told her.

I put the cradle gadget down with my left hand, left the receiver off. She was obviously one of those dumb dames who'd go on dialling my number until she had us both crazy. I got up then and went over to the glassed-in alcove where we do the brewing-up. I went through the motions mechanically; I knew the stuff wouldn't be as good as Stella makes but it would keep me going until I could get to a restaurant. I'd eat out tonight which would help my stomach lining through the week-end.

I carried the coffee back and put the cup down on my blotter. Then I went back for the sugar and rooted out the biscuit tin. Stella had stocked up before she'd left town and there were a few of my favourite butter-nut fudge specials there. I added a mite more sugar and stirred, closing my eyes against the steam. When I'd taken the first sip or two I felt I might live with a little care and kindness.

It was then I heard the footsteps for the third time. They were stumbling and hesitant, like their owner was unsure of himself. I got up and went out in the waiting room. A shabby little old man with grey hair and blinking eyes stood just inside the door leading to the corridor.

I guessed it had been his footsteps going up and down I'd heard before; obviously he hadn't been able to make up his mind whether to come in.

'Mr Faraday?'

It was more of a statement than a question.

'Sure,' I said. 'What can I do for you?'

He looked quickly over his shoulder, fear briefly flickering in his eyes, then shut the door gently behind him.

'I must have your help, Mr Faraday,' he said softly. 'Otherwise I'm a dead man.'

* * *

There was a long silence in the dusty air between us.

'You look like a fellow who could use a cup of coffee,' I said. 'Come on in.'

'That's kind of you, Mr Faraday,' he said. I grinned.

'I try to be. Take the weight off your feet.'

I closed the office door behind us and waved him to the client's chair. He sat down as though he was afraid it might collapse beneath him. Now that I could see him better he looked even more shabby and crushed by life than before. I put the phone back on its cradle. It stayed silent.

'My name's Frisby, Mr Faraday,' he went on. 'Albert Frisby. I'm a nobody . . . '

I looked at him quickly.

'There aren't any nobodies, Mr Frisby,' I said. 'Everyone's a somebody.'

He shook his head, his eyes blinking waterily.

'You don't come from around L.A., Mr Faraday?'

I didn't answer that. I went over to the alcove and fetched him a cup of coffee, shoved the sugar and the biscuit tin across the blotter toward him.

He clutched the cup with his two hands around it and drank like he hadn't tasted the stuff before.

'That was good, Mr Faraday.'

'There's plenty more where that came from,' I said. 'What can I do for you?'

He shrugged.

'I don't really know. I work for the Altair Corporation over in West Hollywood. It's just a small outfit and I'm only a clerk there.'

I got out my scratch-pad, jotted down a few details.

'What do they do?' I said.

He shrugged again.

'There's two brothers. One runs the accountancy side. The other retails stationery in bulk and such-like. I do a bit of both and stocktaking in between whiles, when things aren't very brisk.'

'Which must be a lot of the time nowadays,' I said.

He nodded.

'Too true, Mr Faraday.'

He nuzzled into his coffee again and I just sat back in my swivel chair and studied him. He wore a nondescript sort of grey suit that had once been bought off the peg and that hung on him loosely, as though his form had shrunk within it. His tie was so old and faded with sunlight that it fell dispiritedly from his scrawny neck like it had died there.

I could read all his hopeless life history in his clothes alone. You're getting a regular Holmes, Mike, I told myself. Frisby's face was all seamed and creased through long exposure to sun; California's harsh sunlight has a hell of an effect on old people if they stay in it year after year and even middle-aged people look prematurely old when it seems to catch up with them suddenly.

Frisby had a small, scrubby white mustache that clung like a smear of cotton wool beneath his nose and kindly, defeated eyes. I knew there wouldn't be any money in the case, whatever it was; that didn't bother me. But it also told me that he must have been desperate to have come in to ask my advice because he obviously hadn't any scratch to throw around.

As though he could read my thoughts he stirred in the chair.

'Maybe you won't want the business, Mr Faraday. I have no money to speak of . . . '

'Who said anything about money?' I said. 'You're in trouble, right? So let's hear about it. You said something about being in fear of your life.'

He nodded and looked round the office again like there might be someone hiding in the shadow of the water cooler.

'I'll get to it in a minute, Mr Faraday. You mind if I have another biscuit? I was so agitated I didn't get any lunch today.'

'Take the tin,' I said.

He flushed a little beneath the brown pigmentation that covered his face and made another inroad into the biscuits with trembling fingers.

'What's the exact address of Altair?' I said.

He gave it me and I jotted it down on my pad. I lit another cigarette from the smouldering butt of the first that had burned away unheeded on the edge of the earthenware tray. I feathered out blue smoke at the ceiling and tried again.

'You spoke about accountancy just now. You mean Altair is a proper accountants' outfit?'

The old man nodded, breaking a biscuit in half with the fingers of one thin hand, holding the end of the wafer against the desk blotter. He made a big production number out of it.

'That's right, Mr Faraday. That side of the business is handled by Howard Grice, the elder brother. He's a very clever man. The building is divided up inside, the left-hand leading to the offices; the right is for wholesale stationery and such-like. There's a connection between the two things, you see.'

I nodded.

'And the stationery side is handled by the younger brother.'

The old man gave me a watery smile.

'That's correct, Mr Faraday. Mr Andrew Grice looks after that end. I work mostly for him really, and I also handle the books for both sides of the business.'

'That must be nice for you,' I said.

Frisby shrugged assent, missing the irony altogether.

'As you say, Mr Faraday, a nice little job indeed. I was happy there until last week.'

'So what happened last week?' I said.

Frisby lifted his head from his coffee cup and shook himself like a dog. His eyes still had the look of someone in a bad dream. I saw his cup was empty and got up to get him another. I'd made a full pot. Just as well.

'I'd just like you to know the lay-out, Mr Faraday. I'm talking about the stationery set-up now. It's a small firm as corporations go but a fairly big set-up so far as storage and stock are concerned. In addition to all the ground floor warehousing space where people come to collect bulk supplies, we have a couple of store-rooms three flights up.'

I went on taking notes, the hum of traffic making a soothing background to Frisby's monologue. He shifted in the chair and reached out his hand shyly for another biscuit.

'Be my guest,' I said.

He did like I said and then plunged on.

'We got a lot of metal racks in there, Mr Faraday, because that stock weighs a lot. I was working up there alone. Mr Andrew always trusts me with the keys and in locking up for the night. To cut a long story, I found some of the shelves held different merchandise. This was right at the back. Instead of the standard brown paper or cardboard boxes for envelopes or stationery there were some wooden boxes in there. They had brown paper glued over them but some of it had gotten torn, which was what drew my attention to them.'

'You didn't tear all the paper wrappings open?' I said.

Frisby shook his head.

'I went around tapping them, Mr Faraday. It was so curious a circumstance I decided to take it further. I'm responsible for the stock, you see. I felt it was something which had no right to be there without me being notified.'

Frisby gave a sort of gulp deep down in his throat.

'I wouldn't be so presumptuous as to open them, Mr Faraday. But I eased the paper back. The wood underneath was white with some numbers stencilled on it in red ink.'

'What sort of size was the box?' I said.

Frisby cast his watery eyes around the office as though searching for inspiration.

'You know those long, fairly shallow boxes they used to pack fish in? That sort of box, Mr Faraday.'

I took another note, waited for him to go on.

'In the end I was so puzzled about it, I tried to get the box down off the shelf. It was too heavy for me.'

'So you dropped it,' I said.

Frisby nodded again.

'That's about the strength of it, Mr Faraday. The end of the box split open.'

I interrupted him then.

'What about the noise. Surely someone would have come up to see what you were doing?'

Frisby shook his head.

'No chance, Mr Faraday. The second floor storage area was empty because I had the only set of keys. They're normally kept by Mr Andrew Grice except when I'm using them. The other people around were on the ground floor, in the loading bays. Mr Andrew and two members of the staff were handling things there.'

'All right,' I said. 'You'd dropped this heavy box. No-one else was around and no-one could have heard what you were doing. What then?'

Frisby finished up the last of his coffee and gave a heavy sigh.

He leaned back in the client's chair and fixed me with haunted eyes. He cleared his throat like he was searching for words.

'You won't believe this, Mr Faraday.'

‘Try me,’ I said.

‘Well, this box broke open, like I said. By its weight I expected heavy things like ledgers to fall out.’

He paused again, his lips trembling. I decided to give him some help or we’d be here all day.

‘So what did fall out?’

Frisby’s eyes were wide and frightened.

‘Guns, Mr Faraday! Pistols and ammunition!’

2

'You begin to interest me,' I said.

The old man shook his head, his eyes hopeless and defeated again.

'You haven't heard the rest yet, Mr Faraday.'

'There's more?' I said.

He made a strange squirming movement with his thin shoulders.

'Much more, Mr Faraday. I wish I could say there weren't.'

'You didn't touch the other cases?' I said.

'Good God, no,' he said quickly. 'I knew there was something dangerous involved. I locked the door from the inside and did my best to repair the damage.'

'Quick thinking,' I said. 'You made it look good?'

Frisby licked his lips.

'I thought so. I have a small tool kit there for the odd fixing-up job we might have to do. I found a hammer and some tacks and nailed up the slats again. I tried to put the firearms back as I'd found them but it was difficult. They were in waxed paper containers, some of which had split.'

'What about the brown paper wrappings?' I said.

Frisby shrugged.

'I used sellotape and did my best. There was some printing on the wrapping paper. It identified the contents as being long buff envelopes.'

I made another note on my pad.

'I'm waiting for your theories,' I said.

Frisby shook his head.

'I have none, Mr Faraday. All this is unique in my experience. Nothing like it ever happened at Altair before. And I been there more than fifteen years now.'

'So you put the stuff back as you found it?' I said.

The old man shifted in the chair again.

'As best I could. It looked all right to me.'

I watched my ascending cigarette smoke; it was making quite a pall up near the ceiling now. The cracks had almost disappeared from sight.

'What do you know about these two brothers?' I said. 'You must have figured out their characters pretty well by now.'

Frisby's eyes were fixed down on the desk in front of him. His voice was almost inaudible when he replied, so that I had to lean forward to get what he was saying.

'They're good employers, Mr Faraday. I don't know what they would be wanting with guns. It was obvious to me that no-one was supposed to know the stuff was there.'

I shifted in my own seat to relieve a slight cramp in my right calf.

'And you wouldn't ask them about it?'

Frisby shook his head vehemently.

'Too right, Mr Faraday. I never meddle if I can help it. My motto is to go along through life with the minimum of friction. It's safer that way.'

'You have a point,' I said. 'But something obviously happened, though you kept silent about the situation. Before you get to that, you haven't answered my question.'

'About what, Mr Faraday?'

'About the Grice brothers,' I said.

Frisby put up his hand to pull reflectively at the lobe of his left ear.

'Like I said they're good employers. Nice enough. They've always been fair and decent to me. Though I had a conscience about it, I decided to leave well alone.'

'But someone must have found out that case had been tampered with?' I said.

Frisby looked at me with a startled expression.

'You're a sharp man, Mr Faraday.'

'That's what people pay me for,' I said.

There was a greyness beneath Frisby's brown pigmentation that hadn't been there before.

'Someone found out about that case all right, Mr Faraday. A big man with dark glasses. About three days later he tried to run me down with a truck.'

⋆ ⋆ ⋆

'That sounds fairly specific,' I said.

'You can say that again,' Frisby told me.

His fingers were trembling now.

'It was about half a mile from the office. I was just coming back from my lunch. I was on a crossing. I just happened to look up. God knows why. Instinct, I suppose. This big guy with the shiny bald head was coming straight at me. There was no doubt he intended to run me down, Mr Faraday. The wind of the thing caught my sleeve as I jumped on the sidewalk.'

'You'd know him again all right?' I said.

'Sure, Mr Faraday. There can't be many people about like that.'

'Unless he was made up to look conspicuous,' I said. 'It's been done before. We'll leave that for the moment. Any identification of the truck?'

Frisby shook his head.

'It was just a big anonymous thing, painted a dark grey. It had no tradename or anything else on it that I could see. And I didn't get the number.'

'Let's just get this straight,' I said. 'You

found this stuff, you put it back in a way one couldn't see it had been tampered with; you spoke to no-one about it; and a short time later you're convinced this big character tried to kill you.'

'Correct, Mr Faraday,' Frisby said grimly.

'You're certain it couldn't have been just a case of reckless driving?' I said.

The old man shook his head vehemently. With his grey hair and shabby clothes he looked like a pictorial representation of my financial prospects as he sat there. I could see myself in thirty years' time if I wasn't careful. I shook off the image and plunged on.

'There's more to come, Mr Faraday.'

I sat back in my swivel chair and held his eyes with my own.

'But there's nothing yet to link these attacks on you with what you found at Altair?' I said.

Frisby stirred in his chair his eyes momentarily alert, the film of apathy clearing from them.

'There's a lot in what you say, Mr Faraday. But let's just look at it like this.

I've gone along fine at Altair for the past fifteen years, like I said. I minded my business; I got on well with the two brothers; no-one troubled me.'

He leaned forward, glancing round the office again like he was afraid we might be overheard.

'Could I ask you a favour, Mr Faraday?'

'Sure,' I said.

'Would you mind locking your outer door. I wouldn't like to be surprised in here. There's no way out, you see.'

There was real fear on his face for a moment and I realised suddenly what a strain this old man was living under. He might be talking nonsense but there was no simulation in what I'd just glimpsed on his face. And if he was in danger of his life I might be in danger myself. It was a point worth remembering.

I wasn't carrying the Smith-Wesson today. I don't normally when I'm on the ordinary sort of cases; the non-lethal kind. But there comes a point when it's plain commonsense to go armed. Frisby's assignment might be one of them. It wouldn't make me rich; that was for sure.

But it sounded like it might be interesting.

I got up quickly, walked over toward the waiting room entrance and buttoned the light. There was nothing in there except a few stale magazines and some equally stale air. I opened up the corridor door; there was no-one around in the shadowy silence. No sound except the faint whine of a distant elevator going down. I locked the door and went back to the old man.

'Thank you, Mr Faraday,' he said quietly.

I went around and sat in back of my desk again, waiting for him to go on.

'I think you'll be convinced of the truth of my story, Mr Faraday, when I've finished.'

I shook my head.

'Don't misunderstand me, Mr Frisby. I'm convinced already. It's just that I'm not quite sure that this business is as serious as you make out. So far you've had a near miss from a truck, which must happen to pedestrians a hundred times a day in the L.A. basin.'

Frisby made a weary gesture of his head.

'But you can't explain this away. Last night something happened that shook me in a way I've never been shaken before in my whole life. I rang Mr Andrew and reported sick, told him I couldn't get in today. I've been holed up in my apartment all day, waiting for dark.'

'How did you get on to me?' I said.

'Looked you up in Yellow Pages, Mr Faraday. I took a risk in coming here but I had to have some help.'

'You weren't followed?' I said.

I was getting as jumpy as he was.

He shook his head.

'Not that I know of. But then I'm not an expert.'

He leaned forward across the desk again, lowering his voice.

'I was sitting in a park near my place last night, thinking about nothing in particular. Someone took two shots at me with a silenced weapon. The bullets came so close they clipped the branches of an ornamental bush not a foot from my head.'

3

'Convinced, Mr Faraday?'

I nodded.

'Convinced, Mr Frisby.'

I gave him a crooked grin.

'Though it all depends on your credentials. If you turn out to be a nut case I'm going to look pretty silly.'

Frisby shook his head violently.

'I'm no nut case, Mr Faraday. And I know you believe me.'

I leaned forward at my desk and stubbed out my cigarette butt in the earthenware tray.

'I do believe you, Mr Frisby. Question is, just exactly what do you want me to do?'

'Dig around,' Frisby said. 'Go on over to Altair, see who comes and goes; make some discreet inquiries.'

'Easier said,' I told him. 'But I'll do what I can. I'm more concerned about you for the moment. If someone's trying to kill you over these pistols and ammunition then it's got to be something important. They didn't want the stuff discovered; so it could be something big.'

Frisby sat silent for a moment, his silver hair looking frosty, almost tinsel-like beneath the lamps.

'Drugs, maybe?'

'It could be anything,' I said. 'Almost impossible to tell for the moment. No-one approached you, just tried to take you out. Not once but twice.'

I frowned down at his address on the scratch-pad.

'You got anywhere you could hide out for a while? Somewhere you wouldn't be found.'

Frisby fumbled around in the roots of his dusty hair.

'My sister and brother-in-law live over in Glendale. I could hole up there for a week or two without any trouble.'

I thought for a moment.

'Do it,' I said. 'If I were you I wouldn't even go back home tonight. You got any money?'

The old man drew himself up in the chair.

'Enough for the time being, Mr Faraday. It won't cost me much to live with my sister. And I only need my bus-fare to get there. I can play it by ear after that.'

I was silent for a moment or two, watching the last of my cigarette smoke dispersing up around the ceiling.

'The question is whether you've been followed tonight,' I said. 'It's a fifty-fifty possibility. These people know they can pick you up any time. They know where you work, where you live. I figure you're a person of habit.'

'That's right, Mr Faraday.'

'I can run you to a bus-depot,' I said. 'After that I can't give you any protection.'

'It's okay, Mr Faraday,' the old man said warmly. 'If you can get me to the depot I can make it all right. I'll telephone my neighbour and ask him to keep an eye on my place.'

'But don't tell him where you are,' I said. 'I'd better have your sister's address and her number.'

Frisby gave it me and I took it down on my pad. He looked at me with deep-set eyes; fatigue was showing in every pore now.

'You think you can do anything, Mr Faraday?'

I grinned.

'I can try,' I said. 'I can at least prevent you from getting killed.'

'I'll never forget it,' he said earnestly. 'What is all this going to cost?'

'We'll talk about it some other time,' I said. 'Business is dull right now. I may write this case down to experience.'

Frisby put up one trembling hand and wagged his forefinger at me reprovingly.

'Please don't take it lightly, Mr Faraday. You don't know what you're getting into.'

I shook my head.

'I'm used to the heavy stuff,' I said modestly.

I got up and walked to the far side of the office. I was getting hoarse with all this talking. I locked up the filing cabinets and put the keys in my pocket. I went back to my scratch-pad and tore off the three pages of notes I'd made. Then I removed the two sheets underneath and set fire to them in the earthenware tray.

One can't be too careful in my racket. I cleared out the tray into the waste basket and put an old copy of the Examiner over the top of the ashes. All the while the old man sat and watched me with barely controlled impatience. It was only when I put out the desk lamp that he stirred himself.

'Thanks for the coffee, sir.'

'Think nothing of it,' I said. 'And don't call me sir.'

Frisby grinned faintly. It was the first relaxed expression he'd worn since he came in. I folded up my notes. The old man was on his way to the waiting room now. I hung back until he'd disappeared through the door. Then I went over and stashed the small bundle of sheets beneath the base of Stella's heavy electric typewriter. No-one would find them there unless they turned the office over with a bulldozer.

I don't know why I did it. But it pays to be cautious and I didn't want to let the old man in for anything if someone hit me and found the stuff on me. That way there would be nothing in writing available to show where he was staying. I buttoned the office light switch and closed the door behind me.

The old man stood as still and silent as a statue in the middle of the room. I unlocked the waiting room door and took a peek down the corridor. The place was empty and nothing was stirring.

I took him down the stairs at the side of the elevator shaft. It was more unobtrusive like that and we didn't see or hear anything suspicious. His obvious tension and state of nerves was beginning to infect me now. It was quite dark outside. It had rained a little which helped to freshen up the streets. We quickly walked the two blocks to the underground garage where I stash my heap. I opened up the passenger door of my five-year-old powder-blue Buick and got behind the wheel. We didn't see anything then or later.

‘You want any overnight things or toilet gear?’ I said.

The old man shook his head.

‘My brother-in-law will fix me up, thanks.’

I let in the gear and we rolled out up the ramp on to street level. Frisby told me where and I drove him through the quickening rain to the bus-depot.

* * *

I stood and watched the rear lights of the Greyhound dwindle through the glitter of the rain and the neon-dazzle. Frisby had been profuse in his thanks but I hadn’t taken much notice. The cogs of my mind had started revolving like a pinball machine. I missed Stella’s sharp, analytical brain. She’s a girl who can get to the heart of the matter in about three beats of a micro-chip. If they do beat, that is. But I knew what I meant.

I could see the overhead light shimmer on the gold bell of her hair and the set of her lips as she looked at me pityingly while I was wrestling with some problem.

You're in your Emily Dickinson mood again, Mike, I told myself. Besides, I was getting nice and wet here.

I shifted over quickly and got inside the waiting room of the bus terminal to get outside a cup of coffee. The stuff was served in a plastic carton but it wasn't half bad for such a product and I ordered another and a ham sandwich to go with it.

It was an awkward hour of the evening and I'd gone past dinner by now. I had a problem and I wanted to make some sense of Frisby's weird narrative. I wished I'd got the notes now. There were one or two points I wanted to check again. I'd maybe ring him later just to make sure he arrived safely.

The waitress brought the stuff to the booth and I sat on, my brain cells clicking over like castanets while I made a lot of no-sense of the set-up. I glanced at my watch. I'd check my notes on my way across town. I had to pass my office building; I'd risk parking outside this time of the evening. Unless a passing prowl-car happened along I'd be safe enough.

I went over again what I could remember of our long and detailed conversation. The old man had to be right; he'd found those weapons and ammunition. Shortly after someone had tried to kill him. It couldn't have been coincidence in a hundred years. Like he'd said he'd lived a steady, not to say humdrum life, working for the Altair Corporation. Until he'd stumbled on that cache he'd kept out of trouble.

After that his life was forfeit. I frowned down into my coffee. So it goes sometimes. There's just the turn of a card very often between decisions that meant life and death. The stuff in the crates — and there had most likely been more of it — could mean a lot of things.

There was no sense in knocking out my brains over that aspect for the moment. I hadn't asked Frisby directly, because we'd got a little side-tracked, whether the stuff had still been there some days later. But I'd gathered obliquely that he hadn't dared go back to the storeroom. I might have a look myself some time.

I finished off the ham sandwich and lit

a cigarette. The rain was still coming down nicely outside the windows. It was perhaps fortuitous for Frisby. People who take on contracts to knock people off; particularly those who use heavy trucks to take out their victims, like clear weather and often do it in daylight.

Surprising, but true; in daylight a pro has every possibility in front of him; he can see all the people on the sidewalks, all the vehicles on the highway. Whereas at night there are too many imponderables. But he'd slipped up, even in daylight, using a silenced rifle, probably at long distance, with a powerful sight. But that didn't mean he wouldn't try again.

There were two possibilities. Either one of the brothers at Altair was implicated; or both. Or they had simply rented out storage space in their premises, not knowing what was involved; either way it could be tricky. From what Frisby had said Altair's own stationery and office supplies were in the room. But that didn't mean anything. People with business premises and excess space often rented out bays or sections to jack up their profits.

The people who rented the space would have to come in and out under supervision, of course; unless they rented the whole building, but that didn't obtain here. Which might mean that the stuff was on long term storage. I gave it up, paid my check and got outside again.

I sprinted to where I'd left the Buick and got behind the wheel. It was still only a quarter of nine when I reached the office. I parked in a patch of shadow between two lamps and as far away from the fireplug as possible. The traffic was thinning out a little here and my arrival hadn't attracted any attention. I found the elevator still working and buttoned my way up to my floor.

I found my keys and opened up the waiting room door, switching on the light. I was just about to open the door to the inner office when a shadow moved at the corner of my eye. Then a ten-ton truck dropped on me.

4

Water ran down my face, into and out of my mouth. I coughed and found I was awake. A great hairless face with a bald dome shining under the lamp slowly resolved itself. The slit mouth opened wryly.

'You must have a skull like concrete, Faraday.'

'I'll tell you when I come around,' I said.

The big man in the ill-fitting oatmeal suit put one hand under my armpit and yanked me to my feet. He threw me back into one of the waiting room chairs. Then he put the plastic cup from the water cooler on the floor at his feet. My head was hammering away nicely now and the scene had a tendency to recede.

The bald man sat and watched me patiently. He opened his mouth but I couldn't make out what he was saying.

He had to repeat the question several times.

'I want some information.'

'That's my business,' I said.

He shook his head, his eyes like two tiny slate-coloured holes in the great lunar landscape of his face.

'You misunderstand me, Faraday.'

He tapped the shapeless breast of his jacket.

'I got a piece here that would take your head off. But I could tear you to pieces with one hand.'

'Right,' I said.

The slit-mouth opened briefly and then closed. It was meant to be a smile.

'So don't try anything.'

'Right again,' I said.

'You had a guy called Frisby come to see you today,' he said.

I put my head down, pretending I was blacking out.

'How did you get in here?' I said after a suitable interval.

I was playing for time now, waiting until some of the strength had returned.

The big man grunted.

'Piece of plastic,' he said. 'This door wouldn't keep a one-eyed midget out.'

'We don't deal with one-eyed midgets,' I said. 'They have their own midget private-eyes. How did you know I'd come back?'

'I didn't,' he said. 'I was just looking around.'

The big man looked dispassionately about the room.

'I asked you a question, Faraday.'

'I forgot what it was,' I said. 'Suppose you tell me again.'

'You remember all right,' he said. 'Frisby. He came to see you.'

I shook my head, instantly regretted it. I thought the front of my face was going to fall off.

'Would you believe me if I said I didn't know what you were talking about?'

The big man got up. He seemed about eight feet tall and his great arms hung to his knees like a gorilla. I had no doubt he was the same guy who'd tried to take Frisby out. If I'd been the old guy I'd have been afraid all right. I was getting on the jumpy side myself, come to think of it.

'Don't fool around with me, Faraday.'

'I wouldn't dream of it,' I said.

The right hand came round so quickly it was like a blurred arc in the air. My head snapped back and hit the wall. I tasted blood then. When I came around I could feel it trickling down my chin; there was salt on my tongue.

'I won't ask you again, Faraday.'

I tried to answer, couldn't get the words out. The big man got a piece of white tissue out his pocket; he came over and wiped the blood off my chin. He grunted.

'We want you looking pretty for Mr Fannon.'

'It would help if you told me what you want,' I said.

The bald man stared at me sharply. My expression must have been convincing because he passed a bluish tongue across his mouth a few times like he was a little uncertain of himself.

'Certain parties want Frisby,' he said cautiously. 'I went to his place tonight. He wasn't there. But I found this.'

He held up a crumpled sheet of paper in front of my eyes. I wasn't seeing too good and I couldn't focus. He gave an impatient shake of his head.

'It's Yellow Pages, Faraday. I went through Frisby's place, found the book open, tore this out. It's got a ring round Faraday Investigations. That lets you in.'

I tried to raise my eyebrows, felt them sink below my kneecaps.

'Lots of people consult Faraday Investigations,' I said. 'Maybe he hasn't turned up yet. Whoever he is.'

I wasn't looking directly at the big gorilla but I could see I'd planted a small seed of doubt in what passed for his mind. He put a finger as big as a cucumber across his granite chin.

'You got a phone here?'

'Be my guest,' I said. 'You're thrifty too. It's cheaper to call in the evenings.'

For a second I thought he was going to hit me again. Then he thought better of it. He came forward and lifted me effortlessly. My feet didn't touch the floor as he lugged me through into my office. He slammed me into the client's chair, went around the desk. There was enough light coming in through the blinds from the neons and street lighting to make out the details of the room.

He dialled a number and drummed impatiently on the blotter with his gigantic fingers as he waited for someone to pick up the receiver. I was glad then I'd hidden the notes on Frisby; this character was the sort who'd beat one to death as a little exercise before dinner. And then go on to rough up his mother for dessert.

Someone was answering now. The bald man cupped the receiver with his hand, so I couldn't hear the voice at the other end.

'I'm in Faraday's office, Mr Fannon. He came back. I've given him a little treatment. I can't make him out.'

The big man put his head on one side, looking anxious; he listened intently. The person at the other end went on talking for a long time. I reached in my pocket for my handkerchief and dabbed at my mouth. The bleeding had stopped now and my head was beginning to clear. I straightened my tie and fixed my mussed hair. My suit was up round my chin after the big man's treatment and I fixed that too.

I felt I might live an hour or two longer if no-one spoke to me harshly. The big man was speaking again now.

'All right, Mr Fannon. You want me to bring him out?'

There was a sound like a miniature explosion at the other end of the line. The bald man actually winced.

'Of course, sir. Straight away. We'll be there within the hour.'

He slammed the phone down, came around the desk and yanked me to my feet.

'Mr Fannon wants to see you, shamus. Move.'

I did like he said.

* * *

We took my heap. The bald man sat in the passenger seat, frowning intently through the rain that streaked the windshield, his enormous hands bunched in his pockets. I didn't make any move. I could hardly summon enough strength to turn the wheel whenever we had to change direction. I hung on to the shreds of my nerve-ends and concentrated on keeping the Buick from diving through the nearest store window. I guessed the big guy didn't know his own strength. He could have killed the average man with one blow and I considered myself fairly fit.

He didn't say anything the whole journey, except to grunt left or right whenever we had to turn off anywhere. We'd covered about five miles now and were entering a section which I didn't recognise. We turned again, the tyres sluicing through the surface water, as we rocked on down a garishly lit boulevard lined with bars and strip-joints.

We kept on going for another twenty minutes and gradually left the built-up sections behind; the road was dark now, except for the lamps, a monotonous ribbon of concrete that stretched endlessly ahead. We turned off at the next set of lights and were bumping up a secondary road that led into the foothills. There was a sign a little farther up, where the road split into three, but I couldn't see it in the driving rain.

I was too busy turning left again at the big man's grunted instructions; fairly solid residential properties were beginning to come up, set close to the edge of the road, but insubstantial and ephemeral in the rain and the light from the Buick's headlamps. We were running over fairly level terrain now, in open country, the road twisting and turning round shoulders of hillside.

Wherever we were going, it was well-chosen. I guessed Mr Fannon was a character who liked privacy, whoever he was. If he was an arms-dealer or a drug-runner he'd naturally keep a low profile. The bald man was dumber than I figured him for. I gathered that Fannon had been bawling him out for using his name in my presence. He'd naturally want to see me.

I smiled grimly to myself; the dumb ox had mentioned my name. That made Mr Fannon highly vulnerable if he were engaged in some dangerous business. I rated my chances of driving down this road again tonight as very slight. Or any night, come to that.

The Buick's springs protested as we turned off into a lane with a rough, undulating surface. There were a few cheap bungalows coming up now, dark and shuttered beneath the sheeting rain. We were evidently quite near our destination because the big man was rubbing the film from the passenger window and glancing sharply about him.

He gave a muffled exclamation and pointed across to the right.

'Turn here.'

I did like he said and drew up in the short driveway of a modest white-painted bungalow with a green pantile-roof and some sad-looking statues presiding over a half-flooded square of grass enclosed by ornamental hedges. There was a light burning over the porch now so I could see the detail. I killed the Buick's motor and got out the seat, the rain cold and refreshing on my face.

The bald man's massive hand came out

the darkness and took the keys from me. He kept close behind me as I went up the cement steps to where the house sat beneath the night and the rain.

5

A thin man with a narrow face like an animated razor blade opened the door. His eyes flickered over me and then on to the man in the oatmeal suit. He had a thin black mustache that mathematically bisected his features. He reminded me of a mechanical toy that someone had trodden on and crudely mended but I wasn't in my best descriptive mood tonight.

We were in the hall now, which smelt damp and musty. There was a dusty naked bulb hanging from a flex in the ceiling and the discoloured paper hung in peeling strips from the walls. That gave me an important fact. The place was just a temporary stop-over. A rented pad or maybe even a disused week-end place that someone had broken into for brief accommodation purposes.

'Any trouble?' the thin man said nervously.

He wore a blue silk shirt with a bootlace tie and his wine-red suspenders held up stained grey trousers. He wore a shoulder-holster from which protruded the walnut butt of a Smith-Wesson .38. It was the same model I used and I figured I might be able to grab it if an opportunity presented itself.

The same thought had dimly formed in the giant's brain because he suddenly shoved himself between me and the thin man. We were all jammed up together in the small hallway like something out of a Marx Brothers comedy; except this was no comedy.

The big man shook his head, answering the thin man's question.

His lip curled.

'You must be joking, Matty.'

The thin man turned worried dark eyes on me.

'I don't know. He looks like trouble to me.'

'You worry too much,' the man in the oatmeal suit said.

'Where's Mr Fannon?'

'Inside,' the thin man said. 'He's taking

a nap. He doesn't want to be disturbed until he's ready.'

The big man looked blankly at Matty.

'So we stay outside here all night?'

The thin man shook his head. He had slick black hair that was thinning a little at the sides. He must have been about forty or forty-five and I figured him for an ageing gunsel who was long past his prime.

'You're cracking, Matty,' the big man said.

'It's this place. It gives me the jitters. I shall be glad when the whole business is sewn-up.'

The big man shoved me toward a door at the far end of the hallway. There were four doors opening off. I opened the one indicated like he told me and I could hear the thin man locking and chaining the front door before he killed the light.

There was only one table lamp in the drab room, on a sideboard up the fireplace end and it cast dark shadows over the discoloured walls. There was a settee with shapeless cushions against the opposite wall and on it sat a high-powered blonde with a bored expression who was buffing her nails like it was a full-time occupation. She lifted her eyelids briefly as I came in and then lowered them to the frayed carpet again.

She wore a white wool sweater and dark blue slacks that set off her sensational figure and I caught a flash of fine teeth beneath the full, sensual lips as she smiled faintly in the direction of the big man.

'We want Mr Fannon,' the bald character said stolidly.

The blonde number gave him a cool look. She hardly glanced at me; probably because I was beneath her notice.

'He's in short supply these days,' she said. 'You'd better take the weight off your feet. He'll see you when he's ready.'

The bald man grunted something unintelligible and pushed me farther forward into the room. I noticed then there was a small coal fire burning in the big fireplace with its wooden overmantel. It was cold and damp in here now I had time to absorb the atmosphere. Which was no doubt why the girl was wearing the sweater.

I went and sat down in a wicker chair near the fire; the bald man sat opposite, without taking his eyes off my face. The man called Matty still had the worried expression. He went to stand in front of the girl.

'How about some coffee, Myra?' he said. 'You promised it half an hour ago.'

The girl gave him an insolent look.

'It's bad for your nerves,' she said.

But she got up and stood staring at me from beneath lowered lids.

'How about Mr Faraday?'

'Fine,' I said. 'Black and strong if it's not too much trouble.'

She looked at me direct for the first time.

'It's no trouble at all, Mr Faraday.'

I grinned.

'You'll be Mr Fannon's secretary, no doubt.'

She passed her tongue across her full lips again.

'Something like that,' she said.

She went on out, walking with fine,

graceful movements on the balls of her feet. She was about thirty I would have said and she had the personality to go with all her equipment. Maybe I'd have been bored and sullen if I'd been cooped up in a dump like this with two characters like the bald man and Matty.

The light went down then, making the room even more gloomy and unattractive. I guessed the girl had switched on some form of electric cooker to boil water for coffee. It was something to look forward to at any rate. I got up slowly, feeling as though my joints might break apart.

The bald man got to his feet with lightning-like movements. His quickness surprised me. It was something I would have to watch. Though his speed when hitting me in the office had taken me off guard. I'd been off guard in one sense ever since. The thin man in the blue silk shirt put his hand up hesitantly toward the Smith-Wesson.

'Relax, boys,' I said.

I went over to the cracked, fly-blown mirror that hung over the fireplace. I stared silently at my sardonic reflection, astonished to see the side of my face was still in one piece. There was some bruising of the cheekbone and some caked blood on the corner of my mouth where the bald man's knuckles had caught me but I'd live. For an hour or two longer at any rate.

The bald man still stood with his shoulders hunched and his big fists clenched. He was a real pro all right. Which was what made the situation puzzling. I was thinking of the fact that he'd twice missed Frisby. But even pros have their off days. Maybe the old man was just lucky. His luck would continue if I had my way.

The rest of the evening was likely to be even more unpleasant than the beginning. Which was saying something. I turned from the mirror and sat down again. The thin man's hand crawled away from the pistol butt. The bald man stared at me and then slowly resumed his chair. We sat like that for what seemed like an hour in the dampness and the silence before the girl came back.

* * *

She carried a large wooden tray which had thick earthenware cups and saucers on it; there was a big jug from which there came a fragrant aroma. That and the girl's perfume were the only fragrant things about the place come to think of it. She went quietly to a low table in the middle of the room and set the stuff out.

'Help yourself,' she told the two men.

She brought a chipped enamel bowl over to me. She had a towel over her arm and she moistened one end in the bowl, which contained hot water smelling of disinfectant. She looked at me critically.

'Put your head back.'

I did like she said. She put her lips together and gently sponged away at the side of my mouth. Then she rinsed out the towel, making a warm pad which she laid along the area of the bruise. All my pains seemed to ease away. She smiled at my expression.

'You look quite pretty when you've been cleaned up, Mr Faraday.'

I grinned.

'You'd better tell that to your boy-friend. He'll have me in the same condition within the hour.'

She frowned, looking scornfully at the big man slumped in his chair. Matty carried the coffee cup over to him, waited while he shovelled sugar in.

'We'll see about that, Mr Faraday,' she said quietly.

She turned back to me, working with cool, practised movements like she'd been a nurse at one time.

'And he's certainly not my boy-friend.'

'I gathered as much,' I said. 'I don't think he's anyone's boy-friend.'

'Hold your head still.'

The girl Myra went on working on my face until she seemed satisfied. She stepped back and examined the results.

'You'll live.'

It was a debatable point but I kept the comment to myself. I held her green eyes with my own.

'Thanks,' I said and meant it.

She looked away and dropped her eyes.

'I'd do the same for anyone,' she said.

She went quickly back over toward the table like she'd stayed near me too long. She came back with the cup of black coffee and some sandwiches on a plate. I spooned the sugar in gratefully.

'I appreciate it,' I said.

She looked reflectively across at the big man.

'Some of us are more civilised than others,' she said.

'What does Fannon want with me?' I said.

She switched off as though someone had stabbed a button.

'That's business, Mr Faraday. I don't mess with business. My department is the humanities.'

'I can't fault that,' I said.

'Quit gabbing and bring me a sandwich,' the bald man called.

His eyes were smouldering dangerously. The girl drew herself up, an angry expression on her face. I put my hand gently on her arm.

'Best do as he says,' I said. 'We don't want any more trouble.'

She turned, giving me a secret smile

that the two men in the chairs couldn't see.

'You've a good head on you, Mr Faraday.'

'Thanks,' I told her. 'That's why I tend to survive.'

She put her tongue across the even white teeth.

'Even people like you need help sometimes, Mr Faraday,' she said slowly.

Then she turned again and went across to the table. I kept a low profile and finished off the coffee and sandwiches, feeling strength slowly seeping back into me. The girl was on the divan again now, like this was an ordinary social evening in some suburban homestead. The more I watched her the more impressed I became. She stood out like a sore thumb in this company.

Obviously Fannon was the reason she was here. Which meant he had to be someone of a different calibre from the two goons. I was curious now. I might learn something about the cache in the stockroom of the Altair Corporation and why Frisby's information was so dangerous to these people.

On the other hand I might not learn anything. And I had to tread easily. If a big ape like the bald man used such exaggerated respect on the phone to Fannon he had to be someone who mattered. Someone who wouldn't fool around with a beat-up private eye. And I had to maintain the fiction that I knew nothing about Frisby. It was a fine line.

But it was one I'd walked plenty of times before. I pulled myself back to the present, conscious that the eyes of the two men were still fixed on me with that strange curiosity people reserve for human beings marked out for sacrifice of some sort or another. Or was my imagination becoming super-heated tonight. Probably the coffee.

I finished off the sandwich and as though impelled by some inner secret impulse the girl got up from the divan and came over to re-fill my cup. I admired her lithe walk all the way across to the table. She had her back to the two men again as she handed the cup to me. Her lips barely moved and I had to strain to hear what she said.

'Be very careful, Mr Faraday. Play it straight when you meet Fannon. He doesn't give people second chances.'

'I'll remember,' I said.

We were still standing there when a door the far side of the room opened to emit a long ray of light across the frayed carpet. A tall, elegant man stood there watching us in silence.

6

The big man put a cigarette in my mouth, lit it clumsily, bringing the flame of the match far too close to my face. Then he went to stand behind the hardbacked chair I was sitting in. I didn't like the set-up; I could sense him a couple of feet behind me and he represented a danger I couldn't guard against. I blew out blue smoke gratefully and stared at Fannon.

He was a hard-faced, lithe man of about forty-five with a humorous mouth and closely-cropped blond hair, the edges of which were showing slight traces of turning grey. His shoulders bulged with muscle and from the rangy way he walked I put him down as something of an athlete.

He had steady grey eyes that were almost concealed by long sandy lashes and the sort of California tan people always get when they're out sailing for hours at a time, their skin exposed to wind, sun and salt water. He hadn't said a thing so far, just appraised me with the penetrating glance of his eyes. I decided I wouldn't mess with him.

The ache in my head had gone now and I felt set to cope with normal circumstances; anything except one of those piledriver blows from the bald man. He was something exceptional; only a chamber-full of slugs would stop a guy like him when he was going flat out.

I once saw an old Gary Cooper film which featured some kind of natives who were all kooked up with drugs and couldn't be stopped except for the entire magazine of a rifle. Bald head reminded me of those characters. Except that it would need a regiment to put him out. It was something that required a lot of thought. And I hadn't got time tonight.

Fannon, who was dressed in an immaculate lightweight grey silk suit with a blue silk tie and polished tan shoes went around the shabby little room quietly, like he was appraising the furniture for a forthcoming sale. He was too relaxed to be true. I went on smoking quietly, waiting for him to make the first move. He got tired of his pacing in the end and went to sit in front of me, on a heavy circular mahogany table that had the remains of a supper tray the far side.

His eyes had a smoky quality now and he put his clasped hands round his right kneecap and rocked to and fro for a little while like he was thinking up the opening sentences of a speech for some business seminar.

'I want you to listen carefully, Mr Faraday,' he said in a low, clipped voice.

'Because I'm not going to repeat myself.'

'You'll have to speak more loudly,' I said. 'I don't hear so good since your goon beat me up.'

The grey eyes were still and icy now. There was a definite atmosphere in the room, like one gets on a hot night before the storm breaks. The big man stirred behind me. I braced myself, expecting a blow. It didn't come.

'We have reason to believe you have some information which may assist us, Mr Faraday.'

I took the cigarette out my mouth.

'That's your story, Mr Fannon. But carry on. I'm willing to listen.'

Fannon had a crooked smile on his face. He stopped rocking to and fro to glance over my shoulder at the bald man.

'That's extremely kind of you, Mr Faraday. But you will have to be kinder than that.'

'I'm noted for my kindness,' I said.

'There's a man called Frisby,' Fannon said. 'But I'm sure you know that. He came to see you. We want to question him.'

I leaned forward in the chair, stubbing out the butt of my cigarette on the worn carpet.

'I already told Baldilocks,' I said.

The man in the elegant grey suit was as still as marble now.

'I would like you to tell me,' he said softly. I shrugged.

'I haven't seen anyone called Frisby,' I said. 'But it's my business to find people. I think I have a rate card in my pocket . . . '

Fannon was making a queer gurgling

noise back in his throat. He was looking up in the air, his neck muscles convulsed.

'We have a humorist among us,' he told the ceiling.

'I find it helps to lighten such situations,' I said.

Fannon controlled his throat muscles at last.

'I'm going to give you one more chance, Mr Faraday. We want to see Mr Frisby. He has some information which is extremely valuable to us.'

I smiled.

'If this information is so valuable why didn't your man grab Frisby when he came to my office? You know as well as I do that I haven't seen Frisby. What the hell is this all about?'

I was putting on a good act and I could see the beginnings of doubt growing on Fannon's face. He was talking to the bald man now.

'You are a clown, fitted only for the most menial errands. You could have avoided this situation.'

His face was flushed with anger and I could sense the bald man almost physically shrinking behind me. Fannon put one hand in his pocket and stood up. He smiled at me humourlessly.

'You have put Mr Faraday in a very dangerous situation indeed.'

* * *

He moved over toward me.

'This calls for a little thought. Take him back into the other room and send Myra in here. And watch him.'

I got up too, glancing round at the bald giant. His eyes were smouldering as he stared at me.

'You don't have to tell me, Mr Fannon.'

The elegant man in the grey silk suit had such effortless authority he didn't need to exert himself.

'On the contrary, I have to tell you all the time. Now take him out.'

He gave me a brief smile.

'I'll see you again before you leave.'

'I'll look forward to it,' I said.

The man in the shapeless suit almost dragged me out the room. The other two were sitting where we'd left them. The apartment, with its damped-down fire, dim lighting and dirty walls; the figure of the girl on the divan and the thin gunsel in his shirt and suspenders; looked like a tableau from some wax museum. Like Monogram's answer to The Maltese Falcon.

The big man slammed me back into the wicker chair by the fireplace.

'Stay put.'

He glanced over at the girl. She was still buffing her nails and she didn't glance at me. The big man jerked a finger as big as a bread-stick.

'He wants you in there,' he said.

The girl didn't give any sign that she'd heard. She finished off her buffing casually, gave her fingers a critical once-over. She got up from the divan when she was ready, her eyes daring the big man to say something further. I guessed then she carried a lot of clout with Fannon; that the other two were somewhat afraid of her, despite their tough manner.

If I expected some sort of visual message from her I was disappointed. She was acting again like I wasn't here. She gave the big man a look of contempt as she went across the room. The big man followed her with mingled hatred and admiration in his eyes.

The thin man was slumped in his chair, checking over the Smith-Wesson with an oily rag. His eyes were fixed somewhere up over the fireplace but I knew he had them on me all right.

'I'd like some more coffee,' I said.

The thin man shrugged.

'Help yourself,' he said. 'And behave.'

He patted the cylinder of the revolver significantly.

'Sure,' I said.

I got up slowly, watching the tall figure of the girl as she opened the door of Fannon's room, letting out a long shaft of light. Her figure was clear-cut like one of those silhouette films one used to get from Germany years ago. I'd seen some in a movie retrospective on TV some while back. I stood there until she closed the door softly behind her.

Then I walked over to where the coffee things were, carrying my cup, feeling the big man's eyes on me all the way. I took my time pouring, savouring the warmth and the flavour of the rising steam in my nostrils.

I cautiously flexed my muscles. I felt a whole lot better now; the hammering had gone from my head and the ache in my jaw had stopped. There would be a hell of a bruise on my cheek by tomorrow. If I was still around tomorrow. I'd meet that when I got to it. I walked back over to my chair. It was quiet in the room except for the faint tapping of the rain at the window and the two men sat rock-still, like they were caught in some timeless spell.

I sat down carefully in the chair, balancing the cup in my lap, thinking about nothing now, listening to the blurred noises of the rain, watching but not really noticing the two men who sat tense and watchful a few yards from me.

I realised then they weren't concerned about me; their attitude had something to do with the significance of the talk between the girl and Fannon in the bedroom in back. Almost like their own futures might be involved in it. I didn't know whether the two in the far room were discussing me or not; probably the general situation regarding Frisby.

I hardly came into it; or mattered. I was a dead duck anyway. I'd already mentally written myself off. Which was often when I was at my best. I would have to be good on this one. It was something about being a pro; we prided ourselves at Faraday Investigations on our professionalism. I grinned wryly to myself. Stella would have approved.

I put the image of her behind me, stirred my coffee, sending tinny echoes round the half-empty room. The two men's eyes were fixed on me now. They didn't relax until I'd stopped stirring.

I finished the coffee and put the cup down on the floor at my feet. No-one moved or said anything when I lit a cigarette. I noticed that I had only three left in the pack. It hardly mattered anyway. There was a no smoking rule where I was going; or so I imagined.

The door of the bedroom clicked then. It was so obtrusive in the muffled silence that I saw the man Matty actually drop the Smith-Wesson in his lap. His nerve hung by a hair. That was interesting to know. The girl came over toward us.

'He wants you,' she told the thin man tonelessly.

He got up and went over toward the far door quickly, without looking back. The girl passed across in front of me on her way to the divan. She was turned away from the big man in the chair opposite. Her face was open and frank; she gave me a steady smile, then a slight inclination of the head. There was no mistaking the expression, subtle as it was. It was meant to be a gesture of encouragement.

She sat down again and the silence crept back in. The big man was hunched in the chair, his hands folded over his middle, his eyes apparently fixed down on his shoes. He didn't fool me any. I sat back in the chair and kept my eyes on the girl. She'd picked up a book from somewhere and sat as though absorbed in it, occasionally turning a page with a faint crackling sound.

Of all the people in the house,

including myself, she seemed the most in control. She would have been terrific on the right side. Which meant my side, of course.

I sensed she'd said something to Fannon about me. Maybe she'd been trying to make a bargain with him. Though why she should have was against all logic. It was just a crazy hunch I had.

Fannon and the thin man seemed to be taking a long time over their conversation or whatever was keeping them there; now and again I could hear muffled voices from behind the door panel. Mainly it was Fannon who was speaking; I could hear the authoritative rap in his voice; followed by the mumbled rejoinders of Matty.

I leaned farther back and closed my eyes. I wasn't sleeping but it was one way of passing the time. A long period seemed to go by; it was probably all of a quarter of an hour. The door clicked again then and I opened up my lids. The two men were standing silhouetted against the shaft of light at the half-open door of the room, looking at me.

I couldn't see the detail, of course, but I had no doubt about it. Then the thin man came across to the middle of the room, not looking at anyone in particular. He picked up a jacket from a chair against the wall at one side of the room and put it on. He went out without saying anything or apparently seeing anyone.

The big man had risen, waving me up with a savage gesture. The girl got up too and came hesitantly down the room, looking beyond me to Fannon. We walked over toward the elegant figure in the grey silk suit. The big man was so heavy his footsteps made the floorboards tremble. He stood looking at Fannon with the smoky eyes like burnt-out holes in his face. Fannon smiled regretfully at me, the lips twisting back from the flawless teeth.

'Waste him,' he told the big man.

He went back in the room and closed the door behind him. The bald man pushed me forward. We went out in the hall, the blonde girl following close behind. The big man opened up the front door, grunting as he snubbed back the locks and unlatched the chain. I felt the moistness of the wind that was blowing through the porch. It felt good after the musty staleness of the bungalow.

'I'll lock up after you,' the girl said quickly, pushing past me.

I felt something cold thrust into my hand as her body briefly blocked me from the big man's view. I kept my hand in my pocket as I stepped into the porch. The girl stared at me for a long moment as she started closing the door behind us. Her lips mouthed something silently as I turned away; there was no mistaking it. They spelled out: Good luck.

Then the big man had my left arm and was steering me through the rain and darkness back down to where the Buick waited. The butt of the pistol the girl had given me felt cool and reassuring as we went on through the blackness.

7

The big man was silent as we drove. He wasn't much company at the best of times but his solid professionalism was becoming oppressive. Other than indicating the direction in which to drive he hadn't shown any sign of life either; but I could see the movements of his big fingers inside the pocket of his jacket next me in the passenger seat. I knew he could drop me with one sledgehammer blow if I tried anything so I kept my hands up on the wheel, where he could see them.

I was having slight difficulty in preventing them from trembling; the inner tension of such situations was the most difficult part. I'd be all right when something happened; it was just the waiting that eroded the nerves. I turned the wheel slightly, following the lane downhill, back the way we'd come. If the bald man waited until we got to our destination, whatever that was, I'd have a chance. If he tried anything now, while I was trapped behind the wheel, that would be the end of it.

I remembered then I hadn't heard the big man's name from beginning to end; I wasn't likely to now. And I had no intention of asking him. It seemed like years since he'd first slammed me in my office. Almost like another time, another country. Or something like that.

I'd already used the term once tonight; or had I? My brain must have still been a little confused after the beating I'd taken. I straightened the wheel again, conscious of the weight of the pistol dragging my pocket down. I didn't even know what type it was, whether the safety was on or not.

I'd be all right once it was in my hands; if you're used to handling firearms there's an instinct to these things. It would take me less than a second to be ready to fire if the right opportunity arose. Time enough.

It was fortunate that the girl Myra had passed me on the left-hand side; I'd been able to transfer the weapon to my pocket on the side away from him. That meant it was still away from him as we drove, in my pocket nearest the driving door. He knew I was clean; he'd searched me thoroughly when I was out. He wouldn't think to search me again. It had been a smart move on the part of the girl.

Unless the order had come from Fannon. Maybe he wanted to get rid of the big gorilla who was fouling up his operations. It was a possibility and I worried around at it while the Buick bucked downhill over the rough secondary road, the springs protesting and straining; the wind and the rain battering at the bodywork.

I gave it up in the end. There was no percentage in it. No percentage in the case at all, come to that. Frisby had gotten me into a tougher situation than even he knew; and I'd walked into it with my eyes open. There had been every possibility of backing out; but maybe not. Because he'd already laid the foundations of the situation; by ringing around my name in Yellow Pages. So the big guy would have come to my office in any case.

There was an intersection coming up

through the windshield now; I recognised it from the way out. It was the place where the road split up into four or five ways. The bald man gestured to the right and I did like he said.

The metalled highway was slightly smoother here and we made better time. I didn't know the section but I knew from the geographical lay-out we must eventually come to the coast; it was a rugged area, where the cliffs dropped sheer to the Pacific, give or take a bluff or two. I was beginning to see what Bald-head had in mind. It would, after all, be the most convenient method. It would not only get rid of me but the Buick as well; that way my body might never be washed up.

The big man would probably skirt around on foot and make his way across the cliff-tops, rejoining the coast-road later where Matty would pick him up at some prearranged spot. That was why the thin man had gone off a little earlier; if he'd come with us I wouldn't have stood a chance.

But they — or most likely, Fannon — didn't want to be seen driving the

Buick, otherwise questions might be asked. Like I said, I was dealing with pros; they don't take chances. It's their living and they want to keep on at it.

These vague ideas had begun to crystallise and by the time we hit the coast road and grey and white Pacific breakers began to show up dimly through the windshield, they'd become a certainty.

* * *

'This will do,' the big man grunted.

He pointed to a gully at the side of the road which led off in the direction of the cliff. There was nothing and no-one on the road at the moment.

'Drop me here,' he said.

He put the black holes of his eyes up to within a couple of inches of mine.

'And stay behind the wheel.'

'Whatever you say,' I told him.

Moisture glimmered on the bald man's scalp as he got out the passenger door cautiously, the reflected light from the headlamp beams gleaming on the barrel of the pistol he held in his right hand. I could have let in the gear and chopped him with the open door but he'd have blown my head off before I got my foot on the accelerator pedal.

'Dim the heads.'

I did like he said. He backed away cautiously, motioning me forward. I let the gear in slowly and the Buick trundled down into the gully at crawling pace. He was up against a white picket fence now, which had a DANGER notice on it. He got through it with a quick, snake-like movement. Then he held the gun on me with one hand and tore the fence to pieces with the other.

I'd seen some strong men in my time but he was the toughest. The two-inch planks, hammered home with four inch nails, came out like they were wafers stuck to ice-cream. He threw them in a heap behind him, not even looking where they fell. I'd have bet he used a grindstone to clean his teeth with. I'd been right not to mess with him. He'd have torn my arm off to beat me with.

He beckoned me forward and I eased

the Buick on down, taking care not to make any sudden movements. When I was through the fence and he'd gotten to the open passenger door he climbed in quickly, leaving it open.

'Good boy!' he said.

He leaned over and patted my cheek roughly. I took it as a compliment. There was no other way to take it. He was looking fiercely through the windshield now.

'Douse your headlights.'

I flipped them off, found the windshield plunged into darkness.

'Stop,' he said sharply.

He looked at me quickly.

'We'll just get used to the light.'

We stayed there on sidelights alone for about five minutes. I sat listening to the steady pumping of my heart; the patter of the rain on the bonnet; the low mumble of the engine; watching light slowly grow across the sea and make a pallid white oblong of the windshield.

'Just take her slowly forward,' the big man said.

He held the pistol in my side.

'This is tricky and we don't want any accidents.'

I let in the gear; the Buick bumped and juddered forward over undulating turf. I could see clearly now. We were on a broad shelf, fringed with boulders at the far corners, that sloped gently down toward the bare cliff-edge, where low foliage danced and flickered in the wind. Farther out the grey and white waves of the Pacific looked cold and uninviting.

'Drops over three hundred feet here,' bald-head said.

His voice had an almost dreamy quality that hadn't been there before. I looked at him quickly, saw that he'd put his pistol down in his lap. We were about ten yards from the cliff-edge now and every beat of the engine was inching us forward. The wind blew cold, wet gusts in at the passenger door.

I couldn't think of anything fancy for the moment. My pistol, heavy and reassuring, was about fifteen inches from my left hand on the spoke of the steering wheel. The big man was edging away delicately, measuring the distance to the cliff-edge, like he was getting ready to jump out. That might be the moment if I could manage it.

He was just crazy enough to think he could persuade me to drive my heap over myself. I might just as well take him on here because I had no chance once the Buick went over. The next thirty seconds would be crucial. The big man got out while I was thinking up my next move. The moment had passed and I'd done nothing about it. I felt a second or two of scalding fear in the pit of my stomach.

Then I calmed down again. Bald-head hadn't finished yet. He walked forward the last two yards to the cliff-edge and glanced briefly down. While he was doing that I got the pistol out my pocket, threw off the safety and put it down on my knees, butt toward my right hand.

The big man was coming back now. He obviously hadn't noticed anything, couldn't see detail in the dim interior of the Buick. He leaned in again, his voice low and clear like he was speaking to a child.

'Now, I want you to listen carefully,

Faraday. This is the way we'll do it . . . '

His pistol barrel sagged slightly toward the ground as he spoke. Before he could open his mouth again I had my own piece up and shot him four times in the belly.

8

I flipped up the main-beam, saw the fear and astonishment in the big man's eyes as the heavy bullets punched him away. He fell and rolled awkwardly as I killed the Buick's motor and threw myself out the driving door. I scrabbled over wet grass, kept on going. I had one slug left. Or at least I hoped I had. Any one of the shots I'd fired would have killed a normal man. But Bald-head wasn't a normal man.

I hit a rock somewhere in my flight and winded myself, feeling the pistol drop from my grasp. Three shots sounded then, close together, which made me dig my face into the ground; I realised that Bald-head though not dead was probably firing reflexively, his fingers still round the trigger.

He couldn't see me because I was in darkness and the shots were probably going in the air. Like I said he was a pro; they have pride in their work and he was going out in style. Though he'd scared the hell out of me in the process. If I walked away he'd probably die all right on his own.

But I was wet and hungry and beaten-up and angry at being afraid back there. Besides, I needed the Buick; I wanted to get back into town because I had a lot of urgent things to do there. Like drinking slugs of whisky, showering and attending to my cuts and bruises. And indenting Frisby for a new suit and underwear somewhere along the line.

I grinned at the thought, my face pressed into the wet grass-roots in the darkness. I waited another minute. It seemed a long time. No further shots followed. The yellow beams of the Buick stencilled long paths across the grass toward the cliff-edge, their black borders looking like they'd been ploughed into the ground.

Once something white fluttered briefly through the beams, casting crazy shadows, making me raise the pistol barrel at an impossible angle. I realised later it was probably only a gull or some other seabird come to investigate the light.

I was getting cold and the long delay following the action was beginning to paralyse my willpower. I rolled over, keeping the bulk of the Buick between me and the place where I figured the bald man was lying. I could feel the rain now, cold and irritating; before it had seemed astringent and refreshing. Strange how subjective such impressions were; the changed situation had altered my reflexes entirely.

I got up close to the rear wheels of the Buick, my movements muffled by the rain and the thick grass. I peered through beneath the sharp silhouette of the transmission, clear against the headlight beams. I could see the big man then; he was lying on his face about five or six yards from the car. He must have crawled there before loosing off the shots.

I could see the pistol clutched in his right. He was still moving. I hesitated, then raised the gun. It was him or me. He would have shot me without compunction. I was doing him a kindness really. Even a guy like him couldn't live with four slugs in his gut.

I took aim carefully and shot him in the head. He was still flopping when I was on my feet and up behind him, putting my foot on his gun wrist. The big automatic fell from the bread-stick fingers and I kicked it a yard away. I bent down to make sure he was dead. Then I went in rear of the Buick and retched quietly for a couple of minutes.

I felt better then. I went back and killed the mainbeams. I took the bald man by the legs and dragged him to the cliff-edge. It was only a few yards but I was bushed inside a minute with such a weight. When I got him to the edge I rolled him with the sole of my shoe. He went over without any trouble. He must have fallen two hundred feet sheer to the surf but I didn't wait to see.

I went back and searched around for his piece. I took that and threw it after him. I stayed there for a moment and then dropped the pistol the girl Myra had given me over as well. I had no more ammunition for it anyway. It was true it might have been used to intimidate the opposition but I didn't think the thin man would come anywhere near here tonight. And that way the girl wouldn't be blamed.

Matty would be waiting a mile or so down the bluff. He might have heard the shots, of course, if the wind had been right. I was already back in the Buick, firing the engine and gently reversing. I rocked her back slowly up the way we'd come in. I had to put the main-beam on for a minute or so to find the entrance of the gully and that was the worst part.

I wondered again what the name of the big man was. Not that it mattered now. Or ever. I remembered then I'd been so shaken I'd forgotten to go through his pockets. It might have given me some information about Fannon and the girl. Or it might not. Pros never went out on jobs with any identification on them. It was an unwritten rule. And a point that was entirely academic now.

I smiled at my reflection, dark and battered in the Buick's windshield. I was up out of the gully, the mainbeams picking out the wreckage of the white picket fence. There was a chain of fireflies on the road about a mile off, coming round a long, gentle curve.

I gunned up the engine, felt the tyres bite on the road. Then I got the hell out before the file of vehicles reached me.

⋆ ⋆ ⋆

It was midnight by the time I hit L.A. and reaction was beginning to set in. I found a parking lot and used up one of my last smokes. I felt a little better then. I combed my hair, using the rear mirror, examined the girl's work on the side of my mouth, and re-knotted my tie. My shoes and clothing were probably muddy but that couldn't be helped.

I got my raincoat from the rear seat and put it on. I looked a little more respectable then. I sprinted across to the diner; there were only a couple of dozen people in the room the size of an aeroplane hangar and no-one took the slightest notice of me.

I ordered black coffee, a plate of soup

and a couple of double-decker sandwiches and had them brought to a side booth. I realised it was only three hours or so since I'd eaten at Fannon's bungalow but I'd been burning up the calories since then.

I got through the stuff in short order, only half-hearing the mumbled conversation at the far tables. I debated whether to go to a hotel instead of Park West. In the end I decided to go home. There was no sense in over-reacting. Fannon would think I was dead by now.

He'd go on thinking that until the bald man failed to show up. Even then he might not know. It depended whether the hit-man was supposed to check back. But the thin man would certainly know if he was waiting for Bald-head. And he'd lose no time in reporting to Fannon. If they checked the cliff they might think we'd both gone over.

In the end I thought I'd be all right for one night at Park West. I'd play it by ear after that. Firstly, I needed the Smith-Wesson and some spare clips. So that dictated my movements. If they came looking for me there I knew the layout and they didn't. They hadn't got Frisby and they hadn't got me. I could get the local police to stake-out the place, of course; they'd done it before and Captain Dan Tucker of the City Force was an old friend. But that meant giving out with the information; and I've never been one for that.

I puzzled out a few more loose ends while I got through the soup and sandwiches. Fannon had mentioned some information Frisby had. He could have been lying, of course. He probably meant the information about the firearms. But it was worth checking out. I could have asked Frisby himself; but it was too late now and his sister and her husband would only become suspicious if private eyes started ringing the old man around twelve-thirty a.m.

Today was Saturday. I didn't normally hit the office unless there was some exceptional reason, so that took care of that. My biggest strength was the distance and the lateness of the hour. By the time Fannon had some idea of the truth it would be too late. Firstly, the thin man had to get to a phone. Even if he went to the bluff and didn't see Bald-head he might think he'd missed him on the road somewhere. He could fool around all night like that.

By the time he phoned Fannon with his nebulous news it could be the small hours. And the bungalow was a long way out of L.A. So they wouldn't trouble me tonight. The more I chewed it over with my sandwich the more I liked it.

And there was another small precaution I could take. I could stash the car some blocks away from my rented house, in rear of a thick hedge on my neighbour's property. I'd done it before under similar circumstances and he had plenty of spare space there.

It was nearly one a.m. by the time I left the dinette and the proprietor, a small, scowling man with curly brown hair and his girl-friend, a tall, thin woman who looked like Olive Oyl on her night off, were standing around pointedly waiting for the last three late-stayers to leave.

I got behind the wheel and smoked

over to my section of town in negative traffic conditions, being careful not to jump any reds. I had a lot more ideas to mull over but they were bouncing around in my brain like ping-pong balls so I didn't try to hang on to them; just let them go with the cigarette smoke which streamed out my open side window.

It was after one-thirty a.m. by the time I trundled the Buick quietly up the hill to Park West but it felt like five. I cut the motor and freewheeled down the drive-way to the shelter of my neighbour's hedge and silently shut the door behind me, not bothering to lock it. I dragged my way back along the wet concrete in the darkness and the rain thinking how terrific the life of a P.I. was.

It was all strictly uphill on Dad Frisby's case so far. I wondered if it would get any easier. There was no-one around and a lot of nothing in the length of the drenched boulevard shining under the lamps as I put my key in the front door. The house had that stale, unlived-in air that houses always have when the occupants spend most of their time away.

A couple of bills sneered sourly up at me from the mat and I put them on the table as I went by, leaving my raincoat to dry on the newel post at the bottom of the stairs. After I'd locked and chained the front door, buttoned a couple of lights and checked the kitchen entrance, I padded upstairs and broke out my Smith-Wesson .38 from the armoury cupboard and put it, a couple of spare clips and the nylon holster, under my pillow.

Then I kicked off my clothes on the bathroom floor, avoiding my image in the mirror. I swivelled under the hot jet, feeling the tiredness and pain sluicing away down the chrome grille at my feet. I put on my pyjamas and went over to the mirror. The bruise was coming up nicely but otherwise I looked remarkably normal.

I cleaned my teeth and went back downstairs after putting my stuff on the rack to dry. I fetched a glass from the kitchen and a bottle of bourbon from the living room cabinet and went back upstairs, switching the lights off. I closed and locked the bedroom door behind me, laid out some fresh clothes and a different suit for the morning and flopped on to the bed.

I poured myself a long slug, felt it chasing away the cold and damp from my bones. I listened to a late night news bulletin on the radio, fixed my bedside alarm for six a.m., switched off the light, before pouring myself a second stiff one.

I passed out cold as soon as my head hit the pillow.

9

I surfaced through layers of cotton wool with the taste of stale rock-cakes in my mouth. It was a misty morning but the rain had stopped and slanting sunlight was beginning to glance through. I dragged myself out of bed and went to the window. Park West looked well-manicured and normal and nothing yet moved in the length of my section of road.

I went around checking the doors and then got under the shower. By the time I was on coffee, toast and grapefruit juice I thought I might live another year or two. I fixed up the cut at the side of my mouth in the bathroom mirror and looked almost normal by the time I locked the front door.

My raincoat, though shapeless, was dry by now and I folded it over my arm, holding the Smith-Wesson beneath. It was ridiculous really but it was the way

Frisby's business had made me. I could have rung him from the house this morning but I didn't want to do that for a number of reasons. Firstly, it wasn't fair to disturb the old man at such an early hour; and secondly, I didn't think it wise to let anyone know I was at Park West, even my own client. The people I was up against didn't mind how they got their information and it wouldn't take them two seconds to make the old man spill his guts if they ever caught up with him. Nobody knew I was alive for sure at the moment and I intended it to stay that way.

Similarly, if anyone had phoned Park West during the night I wouldn't have answered; there was no percentage in such an action. It was an amateur play under the circumstances. I was up near my neighbour's house now, walking on the grass verge instead of the sidewalk, so nobody the other side the hedge could hear my foot-steps.

You're a real pro, Faraday, I told myself admiringly. Early as it was my neighbour was around, standing on his driveway in tan slacks, a blue silk shirt and a scarlet sweater, practising golf swings. He was a circuit judge, a pretty good one from what I heard and a man not given to gabbiness.

I thanked him for the loan of his forecourt and he frowned slightly as I finished my spiel.

'You haven't seen me, George,' I told him.

He shrugged, making fancy movements in the air with his club. Golf nuts all do that; it's supposed to be the perfect stroke but I never see them do that when they're actually playing on the courses. Not that I'm ever there.

'Sure, Mike,' he said. 'Just as you say.'

I got in the seat of the Buick, fired the motor.

'Don't take any rubber bribes,' I said.

He took another imaginary stroke.

'I'm not important enough to bribe, sonny,' he said cheerfully.

I saw his wave dwindle in the rear mirror and turned up the road at right-angles in order to avoid going back past my own place. I circled the block and then started making time in to town. I didn't see anything then or later and soon I got snarled up in the streams of the mainstem and was too busy concentrating to watch my rear mirror too closely.

I glanced at my watch. It was still too early for what I had in mind. I had two hours to kill at least. I ought maybe to try to ring Frisby some time after eight if I could find a suitable spot. It depended on how soon I got downtown.

I found somewhere in the end but had to queue to get into a parking lot. By that time it was seven-thirty and the heat was beginning to start. I walked back a block and found a small, discreet sort of place which had a couple of pay-phones up the far end. I ordered a cup of coffee and a roll and while my order was being filled I went over to grab the phone.

It took a little while and I was almost ready to come off the wire when the receiver at the other end was lifted. There was a heavy breathing such as might be made by a frightened old man.

'Mr Frisby?' I said. 'It's Faraday.'

There was a sound at the other end

which translated itself into a sigh of relief.

'Oh, it's you, Mr Faraday. I'm alone here and I always get frightened when the phone rings.'

'Don't worry about it,' I said. 'Just sit tight. What happened to your in-laws?'

He cleared his throat with a low rasping noise. The hopelessness was back in the voice again now.

'They went up to see friends in Encino for the week-end. They wanted me to go with them but I remembered what you said and decided to stay put. They got off only half an hour ago.'

'That's fine,' I said. 'I'm coming over this afternoon for another chat.'

Frisby's voice brightened.

'That's good, Mr Faraday. I'll look forward to it. You know how to get here?'

'I'll find it all right,' I said.

He hesitated again and then came on with the question that had been needling him.

'How you making out, Mr Faraday?'

'Not so hot,' I said. 'You were right. This is a dangerous business.'

There was fright in the voice now.

'What do you mean, Mr Faraday?'

'Just what I say,' I told him. 'I'll go into details when we meet. But you needn't worry about your bald friend any more. He won't be troubling anyone again.'

He sucked in his breath with an ugly implosive sound.

'That's good to hear, Mr Faraday,' he began in a trembling voice. 'Might I ask . . . '

'You may not,' I said. 'Just sit tight and I'll be over around three.'

He thanked me quaveringly and then I put the phone down. The dark waitress with the well-upholstered figure and the low-cut dress was already bending over my table, putting the stuff out. She had plenty of goods on display and she took her time straightening up. I was in no hurry and enjoyed the view while it was there. She was obviously enjoying herself.

'Anything else, sir?' she said softly.

I kept my eyes on the open vee of her dress.

'I'll take a raincheck on it,' I said.

She ran a pink tongue around her full mouth.

'I get off around six,' she said.

'I've got it in my notebook,' I said.

Her smile lasted her all the way back to the hash counter. I worked my way through the coffee and rolls, mulling over the conversation. Frisby was a frightened man all right. He had reason to be. But I had a hunch he might still know a little more than he'd told me. Which was why I wanted to see him. I glanced at my watch. I had plenty of time yet. I sat back, savoured the coffee and took half-an-hour off from murder and mayhem.

* * *

The offices of the Altair Corporation were in a fairly prosperous-looking three storey white concrete building set back in a big lot with plenty of parking space; some outbuildings in rear and separate bays for commercial vehicles, presumably those which collected and delivered the stationery and other supplies.

It was around half-nine when I arrived there and they were open and doing plenty of business judging by the amount of metal parked in front and at the side. I guessed Saturday was the big day for these boys.

I tooled the Buick on into the parking area and drew in unobtrusively under the shade of some pepper trees, killing the motor. I sat and smoked for a minute or two, getting an idea of the lay-out. I noted the warehouses Frisby had spoken of and then the zig-zag metal ladder at the side of the main Corporation building which led to the second and third storey storage areas the old man had mentioned.

It seemed a screwy set-up until I noticed the metal hoist set against the wall; this would obviously be used to lift the heavy stuff to the top and there were two metal platforms with chains round them which connected with the stairways and entrances on the two floors. I could see why anyone who wanted to store munitions there would think it a good place.

It was the best place in the world except for the sharp eyes of a curious old man. I guessed Frisby hadn't told me the entire truth; he'd varnished things a little.

Probably he merely noticed the unauthorised boxes and couldn't resist tearing the wrappings on the nearest open. He'd certainly paid dearly for the knowledge he'd gained.

As to what the munitions were for was another matter. There was no point in going into that for the moment. I had other fish to fry. The remaining question was the warehousing; either Andrew Grice, an apparently respectable business man was using Altair as a cover for something else. Or Fannon and his friends had merely hired the space and were protecting their interests from being threatened by Frisby.

If the latter it was difficult to see how they'd found out Frisby had tampered with the boxes; normally, one would imagine, they wouldn't have free access to the storage space. Although there had been a lapse of some days between Frisby's discovery and the initial attempt on his life.

Andrew Grice was obviously my first port of call; I'd thought out a cover story on my way over and it would do for the present. Grice and I had never met so I felt fairly safe this morning. I wouldn't get to it by hanging around here so I finished off my smoke, stubbed out my cigarette butt in the dashboard tray and got out the Buick.

It was nice to leave my raincoat on the rear seat, though it was clouding over a little again. The bulk of the Smith-Wesson in its nylon harness made a heavy pressure against my chest muscles as I walked on over the forecourt; there were half a dozen small trucks and closed vans bearing the names of various L.A. office stationery supply firms standing around and men in coveralls loading up heavy cardboard boxes from a ground floor warehouse whose double doors stood open.

Neon tubes shimmered in the interior and there was a lot of high-pitched whistling floating back from the ceiling rafters. Other men in white jackets, presumably members of Altair's staff, were wheeling small rubber-tyred trolleys around to the loading areas. The great commercial wheels of L.A. are rolling,

Faraday, I told myself.

I walked on down to the front of the office buildings whose shining windows threw back the glare of the sun. There were green plastic blinds at the casements and more neons burning inside. It looked a nice tidy set-up. I pushed open the big double doors and stepped into the lobby. It was dim in here after the brilliance outside and I almost cannoned into a square-shouldered, affable looking man dressed in a conservative double-breasted chalk-stripe suit. They're coming back into fashion again now and he looked pretty nifty. His clear blue eyes appraised me sharply above the thick handlebar mustache.

'Can I help you?'

'I hope so,' I said. 'Are you Mr Grice?'

'That's right,' he said. 'Come into the office.'

He pushed open another glass door and led the way up a grey-carpeted staircase. On top there were a lot of offices with frosted glass partitions and electric typewriters pecking behind them. Through the clear glass of an inner office

I could see a tall, shapely, dark-haired girl, who glanced at us curiously. Grice smiled affably.

'My secretary,' he explained.

I got the satisfaction in his tones and smiled too.

'Very nice indeed,' I said.

'I think so,' he said smoothly. 'What can I do for you, Mr . . . ?'

'Michael Slade,' I said. 'I help to run a small electronics group here in L.A.'

The last part of the sentence was certainly true because the managing director of the outfit was an old friend. I figured it would be better to have a real cover and I could give Grice a genuine address. We were still standing in the corridor outside his office and he showed no inclination to ask me in. I've noticed that a good deal in L.A.; it's something to do with Saturday mornings. Most places that open Saturdays operate in a fairly casual manner.

Probably Grice wanted to get away to play golf around twelve and didn't want to be snarled up with something that could be dealt with on Monday morning.

'Will this take long, Mr Slade?' Grice said quickly, like he could read my mind.

I shook my head.

'A few minutes only.'

I had my eye on the tall girl in the distance. There was something familiar about her but I couldn't place it for the moment.

'That's fine, Mr Slade. I don't want to seem inhospitable but I'm going out of town for a few hours later in the day.'

'Don't let me keep you,' I said. 'I know how it is. It's just that I heard Altair had some surplus storage space. We're getting a little cramped on our site and I wondered if we could rent some capacity here.'

Grice nodded, his expression clearing.

'I think that could be arranged, Mr Slade.'

'Fine,' I said. 'It's only light electronic components. We'd need only a few bays for starters.'

Grice held out his hand and shook mine warmly.

'I think we've got our wires a little crossed. I'm Howard Grice. I run the accountancy side of our operations. My brother Andrew's in charge of stationery. He's the man you want.'

'I'm sorry,' I said.

He shook his head.

'A natural mistake, Mr Slade. My fault for bringing you up here. But even people who find their own way in don't read the notices on the doors. Come on down and I'll introduce you to my brother.'

He led the way back down the stairs at a tremendous pace. I followed on behind. Grice courteously held the glass door open for me at the bottom.

He paused, a frown chasing across his strong, open features.

'Don't be put off by my brother, Mr Slade. He has a somewhat unprepossessing manner with strangers. But I'm sure he can fix you up.'

'Sure,' I said. 'Sorry to take up your time.'

Grice grinned.

'It's all for the benefit of Altair,' he said. 'I think we'll find Andrew out in the warehouse. You can look around while you're there and see how things strike you.'

I followed him out through the main entrance and round to the side of the building.

We crossed over toward the open warehouse doors. There were counters and metal racks full of thousands of cardboard boxes of all shapes and sizes. Grice stopped just inside the main doors, avoiding the sweating figures in the white coats who were wheeling the trolleys in and out.

He took me by the arm and laughed.

'I'll leave you to it, Mr Slade. That's Andrew over there.'

He looked at me with dancing eyes.

'You can't miss him. He's the original Man in the Grey Flannel Suit.'

10

I saw what Howard Grice meant when I got to meet his brother. I'd heard of opposites where close relatives were concerned but I would never have known the two men were brothers if Grice hadn't told me.

Andrew Grice was a tall, thin man with a lean, lugubrious face and a pronounced jaw. He had greasy black hair that shone beneath the neon-shimmer in here and his long side-burns gave him an old-fashioned look. Though I knew he was several years younger than his brother he looked a good deal older, despite the darkness of his hair.

Ignoring the heat he wore a heavy suit of dark brown tweed and his pockets were bulging with things; there were pieces of string trailing out of his left-hand pocket and I could see the handles of what looked like a stapler protruding from his right. He also had a row of pens and pencils bristling from his breast-pocket.

Despite the obvious differences he reminded me more of Frisby; I saw a connection between the two men in their untidiness and general shabbiness and I guessed they would probably have gotten on well together. Grice stood with one hand on a counter and watched as two of his staff started loading up one of the pallets on the far side of the bay. He turned slightly as I came up and regarded me uneasily.

I put my hand out.

'My name's Michael Slade,' I said. 'I've just been talking to your brother. He said you might have some space to rent.'

Grice started like he'd been stung. He passed a bluish tongue across his thin lips.

'I guess you've been misinformed, Mr Slade. We're pretty full up at the moment.'

I put on a disappointed look.

'I represent an electronics outfit over on the edge of town. We wanted to store some of our light components here temporarily. We're prepared to pay a good price.'

Grice looked slightly embarrassed. His eyes had a shifty expression like he'd been caught with his hand in the till. The more I stared at him the more I felt he'd got something to hide. If I kept on at it he might give something away. I figured he had to know what had been stored in his own warehouse.

'As you can see, Mr Slade, this place is working at full capacity.'

'I didn't mean here,' I said. 'I was told you had some storage space to rent up on your second and third floors in the main building.'

Grice turned white beneath his tan. He looked as though I'd dealt him a physical blow. His suddenly haggard face was inclined toward me attentively. I had to lean forward to catch what he was saying, his voice was so low.

'Who told you that, Mr Slade? I'm sure I don't know where you got such an idea.'

I shrugged.

'I'm sure I don't know exactly, Mr Grice. So far as I can remember a member of my staff suggested it. I think he read it in a trade journal somewhere.'

Grice's expression altered. He still looked awkward and off balance but the relief was showing on his face.

'I'm sorry, Mr Slade,' he said, trying to retrieve the situation. 'I must be giving you a bad impression. Perhaps our Mr Frisby let something drop.'

He turned to sign a chit one of the white-coated men silently presented for his signature.

'The truth is, Mr Slade, I'm a trifle short-handed.'

His lower lip trembled.

'And as you can see I'm pretty much under pressure this morning.'

'If it suits you better I can come back some other time,' I said.

Grice blinked then and put his hand impulsively on my arm.

'Please don't do that, Mr Slade. It really wouldn't do any good.'

I noticed his fingers were trembling. As though conscious of my scrutiny he hastily thrust his right hand into his capacious jacket pocket.

'I'm not quite sure I understand,' I said.

Andrew Grice must have realised he was cutting a poor figure. He made a vast effort to appear normal and affable.

'Do forgive me, Mr Slade. We really can't talk here. But you can see how I'm fixed.'

'You mean you have no space to rent at all?' I said.

He shook his head.

'I'm terribly sorry. We did have some spare capacity up on the third floor. But it's been relet and another load of stuff is coming in any day now.'

I made a wry mouth.

'That's too bad, Mr Grice. My principals will be most disappointed.'

Grice gave me a regretful expression.

'That's the way it goes, sometimes. You know how difficult things are business-wise in L.A. these days.'

'Sure,' I said. 'No hard feelings. And I hope you didn't mind me asking.'

He shook his head.

'Not at all.'

His eyes were hard now as we shook

hands again. I could feel them boring into my back all the way down the yard.

* * *

The rain held off all the way to Frisby's place. It took me two hours of hard driving and it was hot and sticky when I arrived at a small restaurant on the coast road, near Santa Monica, where a sullen grey sea washing up on a beach of blackish sand looked like an oil by Seurat. Farther out, the rusty red of kelp beds made a welcome splash of colour against the grey of the sea and the slate-like density of the sky.

It was around half-one by this time and I sat by myself in front of a picture window and ate their blue-plate special brought by an inscrutable-looking Filipino in a crisp white silk shirt, blue bow tie and a pair of black silk trousers that looked like they'd been sprayed on him.

While I ate I bounced around inside my skull a few questions I intended to ask Frisby. Like how well he knew Andrew Grice. The man had to know what was in his own store-rooms. And his demeanour hadn't exactly impressed. He was a bundle of nerves. Like Frisby come to that.

Of course, Grice could have leased the space out. In which case he might or might not have known what the wooden boxes contained. His attitude to my innocuous request inclined me to think that he had leased the space. And perhaps suspected something was wrong but hadn't wanted to know and didn't want to know. Except he was involved. I speared a piece of steak and stared out at a small sailing dinghy with a red leg-of-mutton sail which was tacking in close to shore, suddenly seeming to fill all the available window frame.

I lowered my head quickly. I'd had a sudden impression that there might be a man with a silenced pistol in back of the sail, his finger on the trigger, the sight lined up on my head. The crack of the glass would pass unnoticed in the restaurant clatter in here and as I sank slowly forward into my lunch the dinghy would be heading out to sea again.

I looked up. The sailboat had already done just that. There were two blonde girls wearing topless swim-suits sitting in the steering well. They were laughing at something, heads thrown back, wind rippling their hair. I relaxed then and watched them out of sight. My nerves would be more shot than Frisby's if I went on at this rate.

I ordered a spectacular-looking dessert with coffee to follow and watched the Filipino rippling his way back to the bar area, his incurious gaze focused somewhere miles in front of him. He weaved his way effortlessly between the tables with the inborn skill of a juggler.

He would be the sort of character who could do three things with his hands and body at once, while his mind remained free to concentrate on other matters. Like learning Euclid or the theory of bi-metallism. I grinned to myself at the table-cloth, ignoring the stares of a frosty matron with a pound of candied fruit on her hat, who was sitting in the opposite booth.

My thoughts were in a tangle again

now. I was having difficulty in picking up the threads. All I had for the moment were suspicions about Andrew Grice; Fannon; the girl and the gunsel who might or might not be searching for me; and who might or might not still be at the bungalow; and Frisby, a frail old man who might hold the key to all this stuff.

There remained the question of whether the munitions were still in store at the premises of the Altair Corporation; judging by Grice's reaction I figured they might be. I'd think about that again once I'd seen the old man. Stella's face and the gold bell of her hair suddenly slid between me and the dull, heaving surface of the sea outside the restaurant window. The Filipino was back now and the image faded. Monday would be a day to circle in the calendar.

The immaculate figure in the silk shirt glided round the table, put the food down, muttered something discreet and low and disappeared. When he'd gone I found all the stuff I'd ordered, plus a small jigger of cognac with the compliments of the management; and the tab, which was twice as big as I figured. I rooted around in my wallet for my credit-card. I smiled again as I thought all this was coming off Frisby's expenses.

I flexed my shoulder muscles, conscious of the bulk of the Smith-Wesson; the side of my head was beginning to ache again now but the bruise was less angry than yesterday. I'd be as good as new by Monday. In more ways than one. It was two-fifteen when I got up from the table and settled the check. I got outside again to find a sullen sun shining brassily from behind hazy cloud and gilding an occasional wavetop.

It wasn't working very hard today but at least it brightened the scene a little. I got behind the wheel of the Buick and wound down the window to let the stale air out. I'd told Frisby I'd be along around three and I had a ways to go yet. The air coming in as I drove, with the sea on my left-hand side, seemed like it had been fried before it reached me. There would be a storm before long.

Fannon was a pro; there was no doubt about it. But was he working for Andrew

Grice? Or for himself? And where did the girl fit in? She didn't seem like a gangster's moll. And why should she have saved my life? Or could Fannon have given me the chance of taking the bald man out and getting rid of a character who was becoming an embarrassment to him? I'd asked myself that before but these were perennial questions.

No doubt I'd find the answers to these and a few other queries if I worried on at them. Assuming I met up with Fannon again.

I thought he'd bought my story all right about not knowing the old man. Or he could be playing a deeper game. But he was after Frisby; so was I. The silver-haired clerk was my client and I intended to stay close to him. So Fannon would turn up sooner or later. Except that I'd be ready for him this time. And I was armed now.

I wanted to thank the girl Myra too; her face kept weaving in and out of my thoughts. I gave it all up in the end and concentrated on the steering.

I turned inland from the sea down

Santa Monica Boulevard and started heading toward Glendale, passing Los Feliz Boulevard, remembering that Basil Rathbone had once lived high on the hog there in the thirties.

There was a good deal of industrial development on the horizon and a small commercial airport but I managed to avoid that and skirted around, reading the route off the large-scale taped to my dashboard.

It was only a quarter after three when I reached the right section of Glendale and tooled on down, looking for Santa Rosa Crescent. I overshot it once and then caught it again as the road looped round to connect with the other end.

There were rows of respectable estate development here with identical pantile roofs; TV aerials; and immaculately groomed backyards. I drew the Buick in to the side of the tarmac road next to a strip of well-tended turf shaded by jacarandas and killed the motor.

I walked back a ways, still digesting my lunch and glad to stretch my legs. The place I wanted was slightly run down with a lot of peeling stucco but generally respectable; the yard well looked after, with some old trees, elegant wicker garden furniture and a porch that gleamed with fresh white paint.

Sun and industrial smog wreck the façades of properties in no time in the coastal areas of Southern California and I guessed that Frisby's in-laws were having their annual painting session; the husband maybe dealing with the exterior piece by piece. I could see through the half-open doors that the garage was empty and there was oil on the driveway like they'd been checking over their heap before leaving for Encino.

I went up on the stoop and buttoned the bell. It made a savage buzzing sound far in the interior. A mosquito buzzed too, like an echo of the bell. The muted sun fell like a dull hammer blow on the back of my neck. That was the P.I.'s biggest hazard out here; sunstroke. I gave my teeth an airing, looking at my dark reflection in the glass of the porch. Ten years seemed to pass. No-one came.

I went up and tried the front door then.

That was locked. I buttoned the bell again with the same result. Then I walked around in back. The kitchen door was locked and the parasol and metal table on the dusty lawn seemed a mockery under the leaden sky. There was the faint rumble of thunder in the distance.

There was a sun-room a little farther along the façade; the lower half of one of the windows was open and the curtains were flapping in the slight breeze that had sprung up. I went over and looked through. There was nothing in the room except furniture and faded wallpaper. I looked around the garden; no-one moved in the humid silence.

Then I put my foot over the sill and stepped into the room.

11

I could smell some faint, elusive perfume that caught at the nostrils. It seemed familiar but I couldn't place it. I could smell something else too. A bad scene. It's a gut instinct which every gumshoe has to have. I remembered Fannon and I decided not to fool around. I had the Smith-Wesson out now and eased off the safety, walking on the balls of my feet across the parquet flooring of the big, once elegant room.

I didn't know what the problem was but there was no point in calling out Frisby's name; he might be lying down asleep, of course. But on the other hand he might not. He'd been agitated and on edge last time I'd seen him. He'd been worse on the phone. And he should have been here to open the door to me.

So there had to be something wrong. He wouldn't go out. That would be crazy under the circumstances. And he had no car; a man without transport in L.A. was immobile, unless he got a cab or a bus. The distances were too great except for making neighbourhood visits.

And if there was something wrong there could be someone else in the house. So I didn't want to tip him off that I was here. There had been a flock of cars parked on the roadside verge farther down, one of which might belong to a visitor.

Frisby wouldn't have opened to a stranger, but someone could have got in the same way I'd just used. I stood near the room door for a moment, listening to the steady pumping of my heart. A pulse beat somewhere in my temple and far away came the almost inaudible whine of a big jet turning out to sea to make a run in over L.A. International.

There was no sound from beyond the panel. I guessed the door led into a hallway. There was another door up the far end, on the garden side of the living room. I went down there, still walking quietly, watching out for someone crossing the garden in front of the windows.

There was no-one and nothing; I hadn't expected there to be but I made my living by keeping my wits about me. Today was no exception.

The sky was very dark outside and seemed to crouch over the garden and blacken the windows. Another crash of thunder sounded, louder now, rolling over the rooftops and setting up slight sympathetic vibrations in the ornaments on the sideboard and on shelves flanking the stone fireplace.

I was up at the rear door. It led to a kitchen with a bright tiled floor, gleaming with chrome gadgetry; the kitchen windows looked on the garden too. It was quite empty as I'd expected it to be but I prowled around, opening up the walk-in cupboards. There was another small annexe leading to the outer door and more doors leading to food-stores and a freezer room but they were all empty of everything except their fittings and stale air.

All the windows in the place seemed to be closed except for the one in the living room; I guessed maybe Frisby had been sitting there reading a while back because there was a chair by the window and a telephone on a small table and some books and magazines scattered on the divan.

I went over and stared out the kitchen window; I was killing time really. Maybe Frisby had simply stepped into a neighbour's house for a while, not expecting me to get to Glendale so early. But even as the thought flickered across my mind I knew it wasn't the answer.

I went back down the kitchen, found myself in another small room whose purpose escaped me. It was like a study, looking on to a hedge at the side of the house; it contained a few books in cases; a writing desk; and some leather chairs. Except that it was rather elegant it seemed more like a dentist's waiting room.

Maybe Frisby's relatives took coffee here after dinner or something. Not that it was important. I went on to another door, farther away from the kitchen and opened it up, holding the Smith-Wesson high and feeling absurd at the same time.

That led to a rather palatial hallway which completed the circuit.

The door on the right obviously led back into the living room and was the one which had occupied my attention for so much time. I frowned at my watch. It was almost a quarter of four now. I moved on down, opening a cupboard at the left hand; it was empty too; like I figured it concealed the supports for the staircase.

I was up close to the front door now. There were two or three letters sitting on the mat. The sky was so dark that it was almost like night in the hall. There was a lot of oak panelling here which would make the place dim at the best of times. I bent down and picked the letters up. It was probably a late delivery; sometimes stuff came in the afternoons. But it was strange that Frisby hadn't collected them.

They appeared to be bills or advertising circulars and were addressed to Mr Charles Deakin. Presumably Frisby's brother-in-law. I put them down on a small half-table that stood against the wall beneath a circular mirror with a heavy wooden frame. The stairway was so dark I was tempted to put on the light switch. I decided against. I went on up, testing each tread, holding the Smith-Wesson, feeling like Martin Balsam in Psycho.

There was a landing about a third of the way and I could see the sky through a large circular window, high up; it was so dark that I had a job to make out the silhouette of the window bars against it. I was just stepping on to the landing when my foot caught against something and I stumbled.

The crash of thunder seemed to take the roof of the house off. Lightning flared, making a brilliant incandescence of the stairway. In the livid glare before it faded I saw the distorted dead face of Frisby.

⋆ ⋆ ⋆

It was quite a moment. When I came down from the window frame I bent to examine him. There was no blood so I couldn't see how he'd died but his neck was twisted at an unnatural angle so maybe he'd fallen. Or been pushed. I looked around the darkened stairway, the hairs tingling on the back of my neck. I moved to the nearest switch and threw it. The ceiling light seemed to make only the faintest impression against the surrounding darkness.

I went up top, my heart pumping unsteadily now. I went through the bedrooms in a mad rush, not caring how much noise I made. Of course there was nothing there. I hadn't expected there to be but I felt better after. I went down the stairway again and stared at what was left of Frisby.

I sat on the stairs and lit a cigarette, putting the spent match-stalk carefully back in the box. I feathered out blue smoke toward the circular window. Frisby's clothes looked more makeshift and shapeless than ever. Death is always ugly but he looked more like a rag doll than a human being, flung down in a corner as though its owner had finished with it. I guess people like Frisby always had a raw deal.

They seemed to attract disaster. Frisby certainly had. The only time in his life he'd meddled in something which wasn't his business, it had gotten up and bitten him. I didn't know what to think now. There was no sign of anyone else's presence in the house; but that didn't mean anything. An intruder could have got in and left the same way I'd used, without leaving any trace. It would be an odd coincidence if a man in fear of his life had died accidentally by falling downstairs.

This was a steep stairway, of course; and dark. But it was beyond belief. Frisby was frightened; he was waiting for my visit; and he would have taken care. I got down on the small landing and went over his clothing. There was nothing; nothing of any importance to me, I meant. Not that I'd expected it. It was the everyday stuff of a P.I.'s existence on a case which involved rough stuff.

I opened up Frisby's worn wallet; it contained a few odds and ends; a couple of membership cards of some organisations he belonged to; six dollars cash; a pay-slip from the Altair Corporation; and the stub of his bus-ticket out here. Not much for seventy years of frustrated hopes and dreams.

When I was satisfied there was nothing else for me I buttoned the light again and descended the final stretch of stairway to the hall. The thunder crashed again then and the lightning picked up every knot and line in the oak panelling. I saw a shadow pass the window in front of the hallway. I froze. I'd put the Smith-Wesson back in the holster but now I got it out again.

I walked down the last few treads, keeping into the wall and making as little noise as possible. I wasn't mistaken. There had been someone on the path outside because the shadow passed again. I was a little too late to see who it was. I flattened myself into the wall as footsteps sounded on the stoop.

I'd expected the faint buzz of the bell but instead there came a heavy fusillade on the brass door-knocker. It seemed to scald the nerves and before it had died away it was drowned by the faint mumble of thunder. It was time I got out.

I put the Smith-Wesson back in the

holster, stepped down to the bottom of the staircase. As I turned to go back down the hall a woman's face stared in through a small glass window at the side of the door. She seemed frozen for a second then her mouth opened in a wide O of surprise. She screamed as I made for the door the other side the hallway.

The elderly character with a bandeau round her dyed hair, which looked grotesque above her white silk blouse and tartan trews, tailored for a woman about fifty years younger, went on screaming. I kept on pulling at the door handle in full view of the harpie. I knew then what song the sirens sang. It wasn't pleasant. My brainbox wasn't functioning properly.

The door was locked for some reason. The key was probably on the other side. Perhaps Frisby had secured it against being surprised by an intruder; in which case it was curious he'd left the window open. Or, if my theory was right, whoever pushed him down the stairs had locked it during their initial interview.

Frisby had maybe run out through the kitchen and up the stairs to escape. All these thoughts passed in a jumbled kaleidoscope through my mind in the split second I went on tugging at the handle. Then I was running down the hallway and back through the kitchen area. I got into the big living room to see that the woman had moved round the cement path at the front of the house and was staring through the far window. She was still screaming.

If I didn't take off now I'd never make it. I went out through the window in a clean dive that would have gotten me into the Olympic record charts had anyone been there to time it. I skidded on grass, fell and badly winded myself. The high-pitched screaming was round the corner of the house now. The whole road must be aroused soon.

I went through a flowering hedge at the side of Frisby's place without noticing and found myself in the next lot. This was empty and I got down the zig-zag crazy paving path without being spotted, the tall hedge hiding me from the Mad-woman of Chaillot. I pounded down the grass verge, my progress muffled. The woman had disappeared in rear of the house now but her high keening went on. She would be able to live on the experience for months afterwards.

No-one stirred. Screaming might have been an everyday occurrence in this neighbourhood for all I knew. I reached the Buick, hot, dusty and with my nerves shot to hell.

I already had the keys and I got behind the wheel, firing the engine first time. I took about a pound of rubber off the tyres as I went away from there. I didn't slacken speed until I reached the coast road.

12

The shadows were long on the ground before I got back in to L.A. again. I was surprised to find I was hungry as hell. It was either the brainwork. Or the foot-work. Or maybe a combination of both. I grinned at my dishevelled reflection in the rear mirror. I kept a sharp look-out all the way back in to town but there was no-one tailing me so far as I could see; though the faint wail of a prowl-car siren at an intersection had my nerves like Maltese lace for a couple of minutes.

But the police wagon passed on its way to more urgent business and I tooled on in the heavy traffic flow, enjoying the smog and the haze and the gasoline fumes that always hang low in the L.A. basin this kind of weather. My mind kept on returning to Frisby. The bald man hadn't known where Frisby was or he wouldn't have come to me. He'd gotten on to me because he'd found a Yellow

Pages ad for Faraday Investigations ringed round in Frisby's apartment.

He still didn't know where he was when I'd taken him out. And Fannon and his crowd certainly didn't. Unless Frisby had phoned someone no-one could have known. If I ruled out accident and I'd already decided against, how could anyone have traced him? Unless through his relatives in Glendale. But his pursuers wouldn't have known about that either. There was some piece here that was eluding me and I worried at it, automatically changing gear; drifting up to amber lights; and accelerating through.

If anyone had asked me after I couldn't have told them the names of the boulevards I'd traversed. Though I was driving safely all the time, purely on reflexes.

There was one possibility that was slowly filtering in. I hadn't given it a thought before. And certainly the bald man's brain mightn't have been up to it. Though I'd warned Frisby not to tell anyone where he was going, his neighbours in L.A. would most likely know something about his sister and her address in Glendale. It was the only thing that added up and the more I mulled it around the more I felt there might be something in it.

But it didn't help me any because I still didn't know who that person could be. Frisby had been alive and well a couple of hours before I'd showed up at his place. Someone may have phoned him; and if they were geographically closer than I was they could have arrived an hour before and taken him out. That made more sense.

If the screecher at the portico hadn't turned up I might have discreetly questioned a neighbour and found out what automobiles had visited the Deakin place. All this was pure speculation now. I had nowhere else to go except in one direction. And I had to keep going now I'd started. I owed it to Frisby. The case wasn't likely to make me rich. More likely to make me dead. But that was the way it went sometimes. Stella always said I was too stubborn for my own good.

When I came around and started

recognising landmarks I turned the Buick into a multi-storey car-park and queued for a third floor slot. I rode the elevator down to ground level and walked back to Jinty's for a cold beer and a couple of sandwiches. The ex-baseball player with the cropped hair and the crumpled white jacket who'd acted as bar-keep there for as long as I could remember, slowly drooped his right eyelid over his eyeball.

That was his method of giving one an enthusiastic greeting. I slumped down in a booth and waited for the stuff to come. It was cool and dim in here and though it was fairly full the conversation was that low, discreet kind that doesn't batter the ear-drums. I drank the lager slowly, savouring its cool goodness on my tongue and throat, making it last.

I hadn't noticed the weather coming on in but it had gotten even darker than when I was at Frisby's place and thunder was rumbling again. The waiters went around closing the windows as the glass blurred and starred. It looked like being a heavy downpour. But it would be cooler after. I gave it an hour or so; it's the way with all these flash-storms.

And it would be almost dark before I made my next move. I finished off the beer and got through the sandwiches, the tumblers of my mind still uselessly revolving. A shadow fell across the table and I looked up to see an elegant figure.

'Too bad about the storage problem, Mr Slade. I thought I recognised you. If it had been up to me I could have found room somehow.'

Howard Grice wore the same outfit as when I'd seen him this morning and he looked as affable and debonair as before. I got up and we shook hands formally.

'That's the way it goes sometimes, Mr Grice. I thought it was worth trying.'

'Sure.'

He gave me a wry smile.

'If we do have anything suitable I'll give you a ring at the earliest opportunity.'

'I'd appreciate it,' I told him. 'We're in the book.'

He nodded and went to move away.

'Would you care to join me?' I said.

He hesitated, giving me a discreet look.

'Thank you, no, Mr Slade. I have my

secretary with me. We were just leaving as a matter of fact.'

It was then I saw the tall, dark girl with the sensational figure standing up the far end of the bar. She gave me a slight bow of recognition. I grinned at Grice.

'I quite understand, Mr Grice. I'd much prefer that lady to my company and a cold beer.'

Grice smiled too and gave me his hand again.

'I felt sure you'd understand, Mr Slade. See you around.'

I sat down and watched them go out the far door. Like I said there are better things to do in this world than what I was doing at the moment. I glanced at my watch, ordered another beer and settled down to wait.

* * *

It was dusk when I left Jinty's and pretty well dark by the time I picked up the Buick but the rain had stopped. I drove across town, taking my time, sorry I'd had three lagers instead of two. It's another of the hazards of my profession. More P.I.'s go down with indigestion and ulcer troubles through gulping bad meals in diners; or living on sandwiches on stakeout.

The mild joke lasted me until I got where I wanted. I eased the Buick over out of the mainstream and found a slot three or four blocks farther west. I waited until it was completely dark and sat and smoked and listened to a news bulletin on the radio. When I judged the conditions would be right I got out the Buick, locked the driving door and walked on down the sidewalk.

There were quite a few people about, which suited me for the moment and the early evening traffic stream was thickening up. I got up to the section I wanted and stopped outside the window of a sport-good job and pretended to examine the merchandise.

The premises of the Altair Corporation sat back from the road dark and silent, the neons from the opposite side of the street making vivid reflections in the dark expanses of the windows.

There were no lights in the Altair parking lot itself but a couple of automobiles still there, which worried me. Either they belonged to warehouse employees or people just passing through the neighbourhood had decided to leave their vehicles. Either way it was a nuisance. And I couldn't afford to tip my hand tonight. So it required a little more thought.

I walked on past, found an alleyway between two shops which might take me in rear of the site. It did. I had a clear view of the area. The two parked cars were silhouetted against the neons the far side of the street now and I could see that they were empty. That left just the warehouses.

I walked on a bit farther, found a place in the wire fence which brought me closer. I stayed where I was, in the shadow, for about a quarter of an hour. I didn't see or hear anything out of the ordinary. I went farther down where a section of fencing had rusted and was sagging. I put my foot on it and the strands broke away. Pretty soon I found I could step through.

I went over toward the warehouse area, keeping in all the shadow I could find. There was rather too much light here for what I wanted and part of the metal ladder leading up to Frisby's third floor area was fairly well lit from the lamps across the street. I decided to try something else. I went around in rear of the buildings, where heavy undergrowth grew up close against the wall.

Like I figured there were a few small windows here; probably in earlier days they'd let in light because the back of the building was some way from the perimeter fence. But small trees and undergrowth had encroached and the stuff blocked out the light from the glass and no-one had bothered to cut them back.

I broke off some small branches that were pressing against the first window and cleared a space. Then I went back along the façade, searching among the rubble that was strewn about the place. I found a small rusted iron bar and came back with it. The window was almost at ground level and the sill came only up to my waist.

I saw the interior catches were strong and didn't waste any time there. I waited until some heavy lorries were passing along the boulevard in front of Altair and smashed the bottom pane in with two clean blows. There was so much racket going on in front that no-one could have possibly heard. There were too many jagged edges at the bottom and I took off my jacket and folded it, putting it down carefully on the serrated surface. I rolled over quickly into the interior and put my jacket on again.

So far so bad. I waited a minute or so, letting my eyes get adjusted to the gloom of the interior. I had my pencil flash but I didn't want to risk using it on the ground floor in case someone arrived to collect their automobile and saw the light. Fannon would know by now that the bald man wasn't coming back; but he couldn't be sure that we hadn't both gone over the cliff or died together in some other manner.

Only the girl would know that I'd used

the pistol if I got a fractional chance. And she obviously wouldn't be telling Fannon. Unless they'd planned it between them. I grinned wryly to myself in the semi-darkness. We'd already been on that merry-go-round. I moved over, aware now of the metal racks dividing the ground floor area up into aisles; of the piles of cardboard boxes on the flat steel shelving. I didn't want to hang around here.

It was only the third floor that really interested me. I was hoping that there would be interior staircases linking the three floors; there had to be because surely the people who worked here wouldn't want to go out on to the metal stairway when the rain was sluicing down. Remembering Frisby's meticulous mind I was concerned only in case the doors linking the three floors should be locked.

I was in luck for once. There was a wide wooden staircase leading upward into the gloom in the far corner of the warehouse; I stood there for a moment, my attention distracted by the ceiling. I soon saw there were large steel trusses set against the far wall, supporting metal ceiling girders. I went on over. The set-up looked fairly new. I wondered why Altair would want fresh ceiling supports for warehouses that had been in use for years.

I went back up the staircase. I was in luck again. The door at the top had the key on my side. I opened it up and went on in. The situation here was identical to that on the floor I'd just seen.

Racks stacked with thousands of cardboard boxes; making long aisles that ran at right-angles to the high windows. There was nothing here of any interest either. Except for the fact that the additional floor supports of steel trusses and girders continued; the material was obviously of so much later date than the main building.

It seemed to me that the massive wooden beams and thick floors already here were more than adequate for the metal racks and the stationery, even counting their considerable weight in toto. The strengthening of the floors was out of all proportion to the load they would be carrying. I went all round this floor, checking occasionally with the pencil-flash, making sure I kept it down at floor level, the beam shielded from the windows by the mass of the racks.

I didn't find anything of significance; except in a corner a solitary wood shaving that had obviously been hacked from an original beam to allow room for one of the steel trusses. It had probably been forgotten in a crevice behind the steel girder when the floor was swept. There was later paintwork too, which had dripped from the edge of a beam on to the wood.

That clinched it so far as I was concerned. The strengthening of both floors was obviously later work; perhaps done within the last year or so. This was interesting and it certainly backed old man Frisby's story; the top floor had to hold the answer.

I padded on up, again finding the key in the door. I stepped inside, noticing immediately that the place was much lighter than the other floors; I soon saw the reason. All the racks were empty, except for two up the far end which obviously contained genuine stationery. The street lights and those from shops on the opposite side of the boulevard were shining through the empty racks.

I got down on my hands and knees and crawled all the way round, making sure that the remaining cardboard boxes did contain notepaper and envelopes. I hadn't taken all this trouble tonight to miss out now. When I'd finished that I went over the floor carefully, using the flash discreetly, beneath my cupped hand.

I soon saw there were deep grooves carved in some of the boards. Something heavy, with a sharp edge, had been dragged across. I straightened up, feeling a pulse beating in my throat.

Frisby had been on the level. I could see lots of traces now. There were boot-marks in the dust on the floor. A number of people had been at work dragging heavy metal boxes out the lower racks. Fannon had had the stuff moved as a precaution.

I saw something dark shimmer in the middle of the floor as soon as I got round the next aisle. It was a contradiction in terms really but as I got up to it I saw that it was liquid which was catching some of the reflected light from the street lamps opposite.

I tried the flash again; the patch was thin stuff, light brown in colour. I tested it with my index finger and held it beneath my nose. I smelt the sweetish-sour odour of machine-oil. Of the exact type that was used to lubricate rifles, pistols and machine-guns; both on the operating parts and particularly to prevent rust when the stuff was in store.

They normally utilise a special type of waxed paper nowadays but this sort of oil was still used on heavy stuff; it would have to be heavy stuff if they'd had to reinforce the lower floors to that extent. I stood up, wiping my finger on my handkerchief. The first piece of the jigsaw was clicking into place.

Frisby had spoken of pistols but there must have been masses of other material. I put all thoughts of drug-running out of my mind. This operation hadn't got the feel of that at all. I decided I'd puzzle out some more ends later. Right now I'd seen all I could ever hope to see. I was as certain in my own mind of the set-up when I went down to the lower floors as if I'd found all the racks bulging with armaments.

I took my time, making no noise, certain that no-one was watching me from outside. I got out the rear window, the same way I'd come in; but first I pulled some of the stationery across. Then I had a better idea. I'd noticed a metal bar such as is used for opening packing cases, on a bench farther down.

I went back and got it and rested it on the shelf behind the boxes, with one end protruding through the broken window. I found as many pieces of glass as I could and shoved them all outside to make it look like the pane had been broken from inside.

That way it might look as if a clumsy handler had done the damage. They wouldn't find out until Monday and I might be a little farther forward by then. I got outside, put my jacket on and circled around the same way I'd come in.

I didn't see anyone then or later.

I got behind the wheel of the Buick and made time toward Park West. I got there about eleven o'clock. I stashed the heap in my neighbour's forecourt and walked on back. I was just putting my key in the front door when I heard the phone ringing from the hall.

13

I hesitated for a while but the insistent ringing got on my nerves. It was indiscreet but I was running out of leads and it might be important. I picked up the receiver in the end.

'Mr Faraday?'

It was a woman's voice, low and husky.

'That's right,' I said. 'Who is this?'

'Thank God,' the voice said. 'You obviously made it. This is Myra.'

I was off balance for a second or two. The blonde number was certainly one of the most incredible characters I'd ever met.

'You made it,' she repeated, like she couldn't believe it.

'Thanks to you,' I said.

'Can we talk?' she said.

'Sure,' I said. 'While you get your boyfriend Fannon over here.'

There was a tired, dead quality in the voice now.

'You disappoint me, Mr Faraday. Would I be ringing you if Fannon were here.'

'I don't know,' I said.

She made an impatient little clicking noise with her tongue.

'And Fannon isn't my boy-friend. Let's get that straight from the start.'

'Just what is your game?' I said. 'Are you playing two sides?'

'Nothing like that, Mr Faraday.'

Her voice was hesitant, uncertain now. She lowered it so that I had a job to hear her.

'You used the pistol?'

'Sure,' I said. 'Baldilocks didn't know what hit him.'

She gave a sigh of relief.

'And the gun?'

'I got rid of it,' I told her. 'I figured that's what you would have wanted.'

There was a short silence on the wire.

'You are a most remarkable man, Mr Faraday.'

'You are a most remarkable woman,' I said. 'How did you know I'd be home?'

'I just looked you up in the book

and took a chance.'

'A good thing Fannon didn't have the same idea,' I said.

She made another of her impatient clicking noises.

'He thinks you're dead. I told him Baldilocks, as you term him, had called in and given me the message. He thinks he's flown out to Seattle. That was the arrangement.'

'Handy for both of us,' I said. 'I still don't see what you're up to. Where are you, by the way?'

'That's restricted information,' the girl said quickly. 'I was wondering whether we could meet. We have things to discuss.'

'You're right there,' I said. 'But isn't it a little late?'

'It's important, Mr Faraday,' the girl said. 'I'm not far from you.'

I stared at a bluebottle that was dancing a gavotte on the hall ceiling.

'Why don't you come on over?' I said.

The girl laughed.

'I don't trust you that much, Mr Faraday.'

'It seems we've got to trust one

another,' I said. 'But I get your point. What would you suggest?'

'You know a roadhouse about five miles down the bluff. It's called The Blue Cockatoo.'

'I know it,' I said. 'I'll meet you there in half an hour.'

* * *

In the event it took me forty minutes because it had started raining again and the road surface was wet and greasy. I had the wipers going double-strength but it was tricky with the mud thrown up by fruit trucks and such-like and visibility was down to nil at times. So I wasn't sorry to see the elaborate blue sign of the roadhouse coming up through the mud and water on my windshield.

I parked as near the entrance as possible, leaving my raincoat in the Buick, and sprinted across to the cover of the canopy. A commissionaire in one of Admiral Dewey's old cast-off uniforms risked a double hernia in opening one wing of the double doors for me.

The main bar was blue with smoke and a three-piece orchestra was pounding out one of Crosby's old thirties numbers like it was new and fresh-minted. You're getting old, Mike, I told myself; I say that on every case but my brain was still so shaken up I couldn't remember whether I'd said it on this one yet.

I picked my way through the press of people round the long horseshoe bar and ordered a white Cinzano with ice and lemon. I felt I couldn't face another lager today. It had been one hell of a week-end so far. The girl came after I'd been standing there around five minutes. She really looked something and nearly all the male eyes in the place were on her. She came quickly through the crowd, looking neither right nor left. She put her hand on my arm, a worried expression in her eyes.

'I'm sorry I'm late, Mr Faraday. I had some trouble in getting away.'

'So did I,' I said.

She compressed her lips into a tight line. She looked like something out of an old Lizabeth Scott movie just then.

'No jokes, please. I'm not in the mood.

And certainly not at this time of night.'

'What would you like to drink?' I said.

'The same as you,' she said.

I asked the waiter to bring the drink over to the booth and we got across into one of the dimly-lit cubicles facing the bar. The three-piece band had broken into 'Smoke Gets in Your Eyes,' now. It was the best part of Frisby's case so far. If the other half kept on getting better I had nothing to worry about. Apart from the fact that I didn't know what the hell was going on.

'I asked you a question over the phone,' I said when the waiter had brought the girl's order.

She smiled briefly, lifting the glass as though she were offering a formal toast.

'You asked me several as I remember.'

'You know what I mean, Myra. What's your part in this? And why did you take the trouble to save my life?'

She smiled again over the rim of her glass.

'I admired your superbly groomed appearance. You seemed too good to waste.'

'I'll bet,' I said.

I got out my package and offered her a cigarette.

'Where's Fannon?' I said. 'The next table but one with the little man in the blue shirt?'

She shook her head, strands of gold hair falling over her eyes.

'You know he isn't here,' she said. 'I wouldn't be here if he was.'

She leaned over the table and put one well manicured hand on the breast of my jacket.

'Besides, you know how to use that cannon in there, don't you.'

I grinned.

'Is it noticeable?'

Her smile matched mine.

'To the trained eye, Mr Faraday.'

'I much prefer Mike,' I said. 'And I still want some answers. How did you know I'd be home?'

She tossed the hair back from her forehead.

'I didn't. I've been ringing since this morning. But I guessed you'd go home sooner or later. Men always do.'

'So do women sometimes,' I said. 'You still haven't told me anything.'

'But I saved your life.'

I was silent for a few moments and took time out for another sip of my drink.

'There's no answer to that,' I said. 'And I'll always be grateful for it. I mean what I say.'

She looked at me silently and then put her hand out to rest over my left on the table top. It felt warm and cool at the same time, if you know what I mean. She flushed slightly and took her fingers away quickly, like I'd read more significance into the gesture than it would stand.

'Let's just say we have a common aim, Mike,' she said quickly. 'I was with Fannon for a specific purpose. Murder wasn't one of them.'

She saw the disbelief in my eyes, went on quickly.

'I know he's a hit-man. A top-gun. One of the best. But I was just there for liaison work. I couldn't see any sense in it. We're both after the same thing. I thought we might work together.'

'Now we're getting to the meat,' I said.

The girl lit a Turkish cigarette with quick, nervous gestures. Tonight she wore a dark grey tailored suit cut on classical lines with a red silk shirt beneath, which showed off the bronzed pillars of her throat. Apart from dress rings on her fingers her only jewellery was a pair of pearl earrings which nestled among that mass of gold hair. The more I looked at her the more effective I thought her sense of style. Horsefeathers, Faraday, I told myself.

'You want something from me,' I said.

The girl raised her elegant eyebrows.

'I should have thought that was obvious,' she told the smoky ceiling. 'You have some information, Mike. Information I need. If we share we both benefit accordingly.'

I lit my own cigarette, feathered out blue smoke.

'You mean I get a cut?' I said.

The girl made a wry mouth.

'Cynicism doesn't become you, Mike.'

'So I've been told,' I said. 'What do I get out of it?'

'Your life,' the girl said. 'Plus a split of the cash. I've already delivered a down-payment.'

'I won't argue with that,' I said. 'What do you expect me to tell you?'

'Whatever Frisby told you,' she said. 'You're the old man's friend. He trusts you.'

'Sure,' I said.

I couldn't keep the bitterness out of my voice.

'He trusted me and now he's dead.'

The girl's eyelids flickered and she bit her lip.

'I'm sorry about that.'

'That's all very well,' I said. 'But he won't be telling me now. Whoever killed him was stupid as well as lethal.'

The girl had hold of herself again.

'But he must have told you something when he came to see you.'

I nodded, thinking things over.

'Sure,' I said. 'He told me things.'

'That's all right then,' Myra said. 'Is it a deal?'

'Maybe,' I said. 'I'll have to think about it.'

'Don't leave it later than tomorrow,' the girl said.

'Where are you staying?' I said.

She rolled her tongue round her mouth and gave me a wry look.

'Is it a deal?'

'Maybe. You got a second name?'

She tossed the mane of golden hair.

'It's restricted information.'

'Where are you staying?' I repeated.

'That's restricted information too.'

'It seems to me that I've got to make all the running,' I said.

The girl ran a cool finger along the back of my hand.

'But just think of all the rewards, Mike. And I'm not only talking about money.'

Our eyes were locked for a good ten seconds.

'It sounds tempting,' I said.

The girl nodded.

'It is. And we only have to cut two ways.'

'Fannon won't like it,' I said.

'Fannon won't know,' the girl said dreamily.

'All right,' I said. 'I'll play ball. I'll get

the information for you.'

The girl let out her breath with a little sigh. She sat forward with her lips parted. She looked a treat like that.

'I thought you'd see reason, Mike.'

'I'm losing my reason,' I said.

She kept her hand on mine.

'You see, Mike, you don't know what you've got. I'm the only one who knows you're still alive. And I'm the only one who can put things together for you.'

'And I thought you loved me,' I said.

The girl laughed softly, showing perfect teeth. A number of heads turned in the dimness of the booths.

'Who knows?' she said. 'It could be a golden future for the both of us.'

'I always figured Southern California would come up gold one of these days,' I said.

The girl's smile was still on her face.

'How do I get in touch?' I said.

She shook her head.

'You don't,' she repeated. 'I'll be keeping tabs on you.'

'I feel safer already,' I said.

I watched her cross the bar with those

long, rangy strides. I was still staring in the same direction long after she'd disappeared into the parking lot. It was turned one a.m. when I quitted The Blue Cockatoo and drove home to Park West to hit the sack.

14

I tapped the shell off my egg and nuzzled into my breakfast. It was a brilliantly sunny day and it had Sunday written all over it. I'd given the girl's proposition a lot of thought and I'd come up with a gimmick. She wanted information. Frisby's information. I'd manufactured some. It covered two sides of a sheet of cheap foolscap and I'd taken some trouble to work out a simple code involving the transposition of letters.

The point being that sense could be made of it but it might take some hours to reduce it to plain English. Which would give me some leeway. Not that I trusted the girl. But I had to have a gizmo to fool Fannon and the others. The girl might be on the level so far as I was concerned; I knew I had nothing to fear from her. Fannon and the thin man were a different matter. Once they had the information they wanted I would be expendable.

The girl had more patience. She was in a different class altogether; humorous, cool and with a good deal of style. She had nerve too. If anything, she was playing a more dangerous game than I was. So I'd taped up my foolscap sheet in a plain brown envelope and intended to use that as bait. The stuff, when de-coded, simply gave a location in downtown L.A.

It was a plausible one and would take them several more hours to check; it was the locker-room of a well-known bus-depot and I'd taped to the foolscap an old locker-room key Stella had picked up in Grand Central when she was on vacation one day. It was a small bargain counter for my life in case of emergency; and like I said the stuff would give me perhaps half a day's grace. Which could be vital.

The trouble was I had no more leads now. And being Sunday wouldn't help. I had to hang around here to wait for the girl's call because this was the only place to find me. It might be hard to take if she didn't ring until the evening. And in the meantime I couldn't go out.

I'd listened to the radio bulletin earlier in the morning but there had been nothing about Frisby's body being found. Not that I'd expected there to be. It was small beer amid the welter of murder and mayhem that made up the gaudier side of life in the L.A. basin. I was more interested in whether the old dame had spotted the Buick driving away. And, perhaps more importantly, whether she'd taken the licence number.

It was obvious that she hadn't; if she had the number would have been on the computer within minutes and the boys in blue would have been around by now. I finished my piece of toast and buttered myself another, glancing over at the Smith-Wesson in its nylon holster which was lying about two feet from my right hand on the edge of the banquette in my breakfast nook.

Apart from the central problem the girl Myra was the biggest puzzle. She was obviously in it for the money but apparently playing both ends at once.

Like I said, a dangerous game but she did it well; I'd try to see she came out all right. I owed her a good deal, after all. And I've never set up to be a judge of moral values. I'd seen too much of human greed and the seamier side of life for that. You're becoming quite a philosopher, Mike, I told myself.

I finished off my breakfast, enjoying the sunshine spilling in at the windows and keeping a sharp look-out as the shadows of people passed on the sidewalk outside. I went over to the sink and rinsed my things, putting them in the stainless steel rack to dry. I went up to the bathroom then to clean my teeth; while I was doing that I examined my face in the mirror. The bruising was going now and soon I'd be almost as good as new.

Providing I didn't run into anybody else the size of the bald man. I was halfway down the stairs when the phone rang. I got to the living room in about three seconds flat. It was the girl all right.

'A lovely day, Mr Faraday.'

'Never mind about that,' I told her.

She chuckled.

'Just the sort of day to enjoy a drive out to the beach.'

'What does that mean?' I said.

'You want Fannon, don't you? I'm giving him to you.'

I didn't reply for a moment, stood staring at a cream Cadillac that was passing on the boulevard outside. It contained my neighbour's daughter dressed ready for the beach. Which meant she was wearing practically nothing. There were a couple of young blond guys with her and another young girl more conservatively dressed. It suddenly made the idea of the beach seem extremely desirable.

'Are you setting me up?' I said.

There was asperity in the girl's voice.

'If I'd wanted to do that, Mike, Fannon would have been to your place before now, wouldn't he? You haven't seen him, have you?'

'You made your point,' I said. 'What's the story?'

'Fannon and Matty are holed-up in a beach-house over on Pacific Palisades. I'll give you the address in a moment.'

'Just the two?' I said.

'Just the two.'

'Where will you be?' I said.

She laughed again.

'Around, like always. You got the information I asked for?'

'I'm in process of getting it,' I said.

'You're a good boy.'

'We'll see how I come out at the beach-house first,' I said. 'I wouldn't like them to be waiting for me.'

'They won't know you're coming, Mike,' the girl insisted. 'I can guarantee that. Best to go after lunch.'

'Why is that?' I said.

I couldn't keep the suspicion out of my voice. The girl made another faint clicking noise. It was a habit of hers. It could have grown on me if she'd been present in the room but it was merely irritating now.

'Because I say so. Just trust me. I happen to know they'll definitely be there after three o'clock. You sure you got that information safe?'

'I'll leave it to you in my will,' I said. 'When do we meet?'

'After you see Fannon,' Myra said. 'You

want to even the score, don't you?'

'I want some more information,' I said.

'I can supply that when the time comes. Here's the address.'

She gave it to me and I took it down on the margin of a newspaper that was lying on the table near the phone. She gave me instructions how to get there.

'Just make sure I'm not expected,' I said.

The girl sighed.

'Fannon thinks you're dead, Mike. I can't give it straighter to you than that.'

'All right, Myra,' I said. 'I'll buy it just this once.'

'You won't regret it,' she promised.

'When do we meet?' I repeated. 'And where?'

'I'll be in touch with you tonight. If you're in around eight o'clock.'

'I'll be back by then,' I said. 'If not you'll have to contact me by planchette.'

She laughed again and put the phone down. Some high-stepper. I frowned at the wallpaper and put the phone down myself. This was a hell of a way to make a living.

* * *

I reached Pacific Palisades soon after two o'clock, giving me plenty of time to reach the section I wanted. I got down on to the beach-road in the end and tooled along, watching the people on the shore, the sail-boats that dotted the water and the traffic stream passing to and from the direction of Santa Barbara on the Pacific Coast Highway.

I had the location fairly well in my mind and stashed the car in a lot next to a restaurant that was cantilevered out over the shore, giving a fine view of the kelp beds and the diving gulls. I went up on the board-walk area with its wooden tables and big blue umbrellas and ordered a pot of coffee, a sandwich and a dish of ice-cream from a jazzy brown-haired number who appeared to be wearing a sky-blue silk pyjama suit.

I fooled away half an hour agreeably and it was just twenty-five to three when I set out to walk along the beach in the direction I wanted, the sun heavy on my head, the sea-wind on my face and the

Smith-Wesson making a faint pressure against my chest muscles. I'd worked it out pretty well. The girl had given me a fair description and I spotted the house across the dunes about a quarter of a mile before I got to it.

Some eccentric had built it in the twenties in the form of a Swiss-style chateau and it had a grey tiled roof and prominent mansard windows. As I drew closer, still on the seaward side, it turned out to be pretty well neglected, with paint peeling from the shutters. There were two cars outside, one a grey Dodge, the other a black Chevy, so the girl's information had been right.

I sat down in a grassy area in back of the dunes, out of sight of the house, and thought out my strategy. There was one point in my favour; if the girl had been speaking the truth, Fannon and his companion thought I was dead. So they wouldn't be expecting me. Even so I wasn't taking any chances. The second point was that all the windows of the house on the seaward side were shuttered.

So that would be the best approach.

They'd shifted the stuff from the Altair warehouse; which might mean they'd moved it here. It would be a pretty good place. There were no houses directly opposite the mansion which stood on its own on this section of beach; and there was a small rear drive which looped around the property, leading to a garage entrance in back.

The central situation was still obscure so far as I was concerned; the girl had mentioned something about Frisby having information they needed. But they couldn't be waiting for word from Frisby because Fannon had obviously taken him out. That was the only thing that made sense in that area.

I remembered the confusion and suspicion in Andrew Grice's eyes; he was obviously involved but I didn't figure him for a dangerous character; merely a greedy accomplice. I shoved the thought to the back of my mind together with all the littered debris of the case and got quickly across the edge of the dunes, keeping down below eye level, the sea making a soothing noise at my back.

I was dead opposite the house now and I made quick time toward it, dipping down into the dunes and keeping as low a profile as possible. In another five minutes I was only a hundred yards off and stopped to check the situation. The two automobiles were out of sight and all I could see was the faded white mass of the beach-house, with its grey, Swiss-style tiles; a terrace which looked bleak and deserted; and the blank, shuttered façade facing the sea.

To the right was a series of long, low buildings. I knew the nearest was the garage because I could see that when I was viewing it from an extreme angle farther round the shore; the black Chevy had been half-in, half-out the open doors, with the driving seat shaded from the sun. There was a large wooden door in the back wall and I got across to it at a fast sprint, my shadow stencilled black and sharp against the muddy white surface.

Far out, tiny pin-like figures gambolled at the edge of the surf. No-one would take any heed of me, even if they noticed me at such a distance. I tried the wooden door. Like I figured, it was locked. I went back round the end of the building, keeping in the shade and turning at right-angles toward the front of the garage. I was taking a risk but I had no other choice. I kept low, took a quick glance inside the black Chevy. There was no-one in it.

Then I was in the warm interior of the big, concrete-floored garage. I saw why the vehicles weren't parked inside. Nearly all the available space was taken up with big wooden crates; there were some flat metal boxes too, but I had no time to go into all that now. I noticed some had stencilled hieroglyphs on the side; some were labelled Farm Machinery. The latter labels were merely pieces of white card stapled on to the wood, the lettering roughly done with a felt-nib pen.

There was a space of about two feet between the crates and the garage wall and I went around it cautiously, the Smith-Wesson out, listening for any sound above the faint fretting of the hot wind that was blowing in from the dunes.

I went right the way round the garage

in a U-shape; I knew now why Altair's place had been so heavily buttressed. There weren't just pistols or rifles or ammunition involved here; maybe something far heavier and more lethal. I was back up against the side wall now, the one nearest the house. That had a door in it.

It was locked but there was a key in it and I went through into a dim, shadowy place that was obviously used as a workshop; it had benches, lathes and other equipment, including some fairly sophisticated and expensive light engineering machinery. There was no-one around and I walked across a floor littered with wood shavings and metal swarf, being careful where I put my feet and doing my best not to make any unnecessary noise.

I was making for another door in the far wall. This was more polished and elaborate; made of better wood than the one leading to the garage and I hoped it might give on to the interior of the house. It was certain I couldn't ring the bell; and it was impossible to break in one of the shuttered windows without rousing the occupants.

My nerves did a nose-dive when I saw there was no key in the lock. This door would unlock from the house side, obviously. A thin trail of perspiration ran down my cheek as I tried the handle. The door opened into the workshop with an almost inaudible click.

There were concrete steps leading upward into the semi-darkness. I went up them slowly, one at a time, holding the Smith-Wesson down low at my side.

I'd only gone a couple of yards when I heard the faint mumble of voices.

15

They were louder as I cautiously eased open the door at the top of the flight. I was in a big kitchen, cool and dim, shuttered from the glare of the sun. It was empty and I went on in, closing the stairs door softly behind me. I went on down toward the kitchen door, which was standing ajar, walking quietly on the balls of my feet.

I was almost up to it when there came the quick clatter of shoes on tiling. I got behind the door when it was opened roughly, almost in my face. The thin man called Matty came in, blinking in the dimness. He still wore the blue shirt and the pistol in the shoulder harness. He was humming softly to himself as he went across to the ice-box in the corner. He didn't bother to switch on the lights.

He was just opening the door and hadn't even heard me behind him, when I caught him with the Smith-Wesson barrel behind the ear with all the strength I could muster. He was out before he'd finished his grunt of surprise. I was lowering him to the floor, reaching for his holster when a voice spoke.

I recognised it as Fannon's. It was soft and languid but it still had the note of command in it.

'Are you going to be all day with that beer?'

I let the thin man go, reached out for the two cans on the top shelf inside the ice-box. I slammed the door shut and went back toward the kitchen entrance, trying to make my footsteps sound as much like the thin man's as possible.

I crossed a small corridor. Through the half-open door opposite I could see sunlight spilling in through long windows at the front of the house. Fannon was sitting in the vast living room on a leather divan up near the big stone fireplace with his back to me, messing around with a briefcase and a sheaf of papers. There was no-one else about so I knew then the girl had been on the level. So far as this was concerned, of course.

There were two empty lager glasses on the table, some salted peanuts and other stuff in dishes scattered about; and a couple of empty beer cans. I handed one of the new cans to Fannon. He took it over his shoulder, without even looking up. Fannon looked very dapper in a white silk suit with narrow stripes and a blue bow tie which stood out brilliantly against his cream silk shirt.

He stiffened as I put the Smith-Wesson barrel up against the back of his head.

'No monkeying around or I get to blow your ass off,' I said.

His nerves must have gone to the ceiling and back in two seconds even but his voice was still steady when he spoke. I had to admire his style.

'I don't keep it up there, Mr Faraday.'

'It's just the principle,' I said.

I kept behind him and ran my free hand over the front of his jacket and beneath his armpits. He seemed to be clean. I stepped away and walked around the divan, sitting down on the edge of the table where I could keep my eye on him.

Fannon had recovered himself now. He

broke open the seal on his can and poured the lager into his glass without a tremor of his fingers. I watched him carefully, the Smith-Wesson level on his gut but he didn't try anything. He raised his glass in mock-salute, took a few mouthfuls of the contents and put it down on the arm of the divan at his side. I pushed the table back a little farther while he was doing that. I was well clear of him now.

He looked at me levelly.

'I thought you were dead, Mr Faraday.'

'The report of my death was greatly exaggerated,' I said.

He gave a hard smile.

'Does that mean Corcoran won't be coming back?'

'If you're talking about Baldilocks,' I said, 'you assume correctly.'

Fannon nodded faintly as though we were discussing some abstruse philosophical point.

'What happened?'

'He went over a cliff,' I said.

The tall man made a faint clicking noise with his tongue against his teeth.

'That was careless of him,' he told the ceiling.

He gave me a few millimetres of his bridgework again.

'No last message for me?'

I grinned.

'There wasn't time.'

He moved slightly on the divan and I brought the Smith-Wesson barrel up quickly.

'You may have a chance to discuss things with him personally if you get fancy.'

He stared at me like he hadn't heard me.

'What happened to Matty?' he said mildly.

'He'll live,' I told him. 'Your help doesn't seem to be very competent.'

Fannon shrugged.

'It's a sign of the times, Mr Faraday. One has to make do with the talent available. The brainy people don't want to soil their hands. And those at the hard end are short on the intellectual side. It's a vicious circle.'

'My heart bleeds for you,' I said. 'But

right now I want some answers.'

Fannon leaned back on the divan and examined his nails.

'How did you know we were here?'

'I'm very good at reading tea-leaves,' I told him. 'I still want the answers.'

'You may ask, Mr Faraday, but I don't guarantee the replies.'

'I'll get them,' I promised him. 'If I have to beat it out of you.'

His dead eyes swivelled toward me slowly, held mine.

'I would not advise it, Mr Faraday,' he said softly.

I got up, tightening my finger on the trigger. I saw sweat suddenly start out on his forehead.

'You dragged me into this,' I said. 'I'm tired of being threatened, beaten-up and half-killed. Frankly, I don't mind taking you out as well as your hired thugs. The police would probably give me some sort of medal. I asked you for some answers. And I'm giving you exactly fifteen seconds to come up with something.'

Fannon's eyes were still fixed on mine but his complexion had gone a mottled grey beneath the tan. He forced a crooked smile.

'Just exactly what is it you wish to know?'

* * *

I opened up the can of lager and drank direct from it, still keeping the gun barrel aligned on Fannon's gut. His steady grey eyes were a muddy colour now and there was more silver along the edges of the close-cropped blond hair than I'd remembered. The mouth wasn't humorous any more either.

'Let me spell some of it out for you if you're so shy,' I said. 'You're running guns and large-scale munitions, right? There's obviously a lot of money involved. The garage out there is full of stuff shifted from Altair's warehouse. Who the guns are for and why I don't yet know.'

Fannon smiled thinly, his hands in his lap.

'You're doing fine,' he said. 'You don't need to question me.'

I put the Smith-Wesson barrel forward and lined it up on his right eye. He squirmed a little then. It was maybe a sadistic thing for me to do but I'd had enough. Fannon sensed that because he made a big effort to be a little more accommodating in his manner.

'I'm going to question you, Mr Fannon,' I said. 'And I'm going to get the answers.'

He shrugged.

'All right. What is it you want to know?'

'Where's the stuff going?' I said.

'Middle East,' he said. 'I don't know exactly where. We're just a channel.'

'That's fair enough,' I said. 'A lot of money?'

He nodded.

'A lot of money, Mr Faraday. Big people. They don't mind dying for a cause. So we do things right. If anyone falls down on the job they go out. Otherwise we might get chopped ourselves.'

He smiled briefly.

'Frisby tried to mess with the big league. He was just a little shabby man who poked his nose in. He'd confided in you. So we had to take steps.'

I bit back my next question. It would have involved the girl. I wasn't thinking right this afternoon. And Fannon still had a lot of answers I wanted.

'You leased warehouse space from Andrew Grice,' I said. 'So he was in on it. Frisby found the stuff. So you could simply have shifted it. Why kill him?'

Fannon's grey eyes were deep and impenetrable now.

'You don't understand, Mr Faraday,' he said gently. 'We thought we knew where to lay our hands on Frisby. But he seems to have gone to ground. So we're hung up.'

'I still don't get you,' I said.

I squeezed back on the trigger and lowered the gun slightly. Fannon seemed to come slightly unglued. His figure almost visibly shrank on the divan and I could see his fingers trembling. He realised how close he'd come to it.

Emotion was eroding the edges of his voice now.

'I'll try and spell it out for you, Mr

Faraday. Frisby took off with something we need. That's why we're still here. Otherwise the stuff would have been shifted on before now.'

I stared at him, trying to digest the information. I was on the wrong tack; maybe my brain was still addled with the beating I'd had. It had been a pretty busy week-end come to think of it.

'You're waiting for the man with the money?' I said.

Fannon's voice was beginning to get weary.

'The man is here with the money, Mr Faraday. That's our trouble. He wants his goods. And we can't yet give them to him.'

He moved again on the divan, his knuckles showing white as he clenched his hands.

'It's a dangerous situation. For all of us.'

He was recovering something of his old manner now.

'We've gotten ourselves into this corner, Faraday. All right, so I tried to take you out. You would have done the same in my place.'

'Maybe,' I said. 'But I was in my place.'

Fannon gave a brief, wolfish smile. It was the smile of one professional to another when the chips were falling the wrong way.

'We're short-staffed now. That's your doing. Can I offer you an alliance? It's maybe an uneasy one. But it's all we've got.'

I shook my head.

'No deal. I don't want to be shot in the back.'

'No problem,' Fannon said. 'Why not simply produce Frisby. And the goods. We can work the deal long distance.'

I didn't know what the hell he was talking about but I decided to play him along.

'You could have said this before you ordered me topped,' I said.

Fannon made a convulsive movement on the divan and then a large gesture in the air with his right hand. I froze it with a half-circle of the Smith-Wesson barrel.

'I just can't get through to you, Mr Faraday. We had no problem then. We didn't know you had Frisby stashed away. Or we would have dealt with you properly.'

'Gentleman to gentleman,' I said. 'Regular business practice.'

Fannon looked hurt.

'There's no need to be sarcastic, Mr Faraday.'

I almost laughed out loud but there was no time. I held the gun on him, looking out through the big windows at the normal world of sunshine and trees the other side of the road, where old ladies were walking their poodles and old gentlemen with silver hair jogging their way to the beach.

'I don't think we can do business, Mr Fannon,' I said. 'I'm taking you in.'

He had his lips tightly compressed now, his eyes glancing swiftly about the room.

'I don't think you can do that, Mr Faraday,' he said slowly.

'We'll see,' I told him. 'Where does the girl come in?'

He drew his breath with a thin hissing noise.

'You leave her out of this.'

'She's already in it,' I said. 'I'd like to have a talk with her.'

'No doubt,' Fannon said.

He looked a different figure from the confident man in the white suit who'd sat there on the divan a few minutes before; now his nerves made ugly tics of his mouth and face muscles as he slumped among the debris of his briefcase and the scattered papers. Even his bow tie seemed to have wilted. But I didn't underestimate him for one second.

'How about a trade?' I suggested. 'I want Myra. You want Frisby. It seems to me there's some grounds for agreement there.'

Fannon had his head on one side now like he was thinking hard.

'You may have something,' he said slowly.

He drummed with nervous fingers on the papers at his side.

'But the situation may change at any moment.'

I got up from the table.

'It may,' I told him. 'For example, you may get perforated if you don't keep the right side of my temper.'

Fannon got up too. His face was grey and twisted now. He looked desperately over toward the half-open doorway of the living room. That was when the thin man appeared and started pumping shots in our direction.

16

A mirror shattered in rear somewhere as I dived across the table, hit the carpet and rolled over heavily. I was in the shelter of a davenport and brought the Smith-Wesson up. The shot was high and plaster rained from the wall a yard from the doorway. But Matty was almost out of ammunition already. He was coming across the room at a shambling run and my aim was steady.

My first shot caught him in the shoulder and punched him away. His cannon thumped to the carpet and rolled somewhere. I was already moving on; Fannon had got to the briefcase, was rummaging around inside it like a crazy man. Flame erupted from the bottom of the case and scraps of leather flew every which way as the heavy slug slammed through.

It hit the ceiling and clouds of plaster descended, mingling with heavy blue plumes of smoke. It was like world war three in here. Matty was almost up to me now. He had a knife from somewhere. I got him through the gut while he was changing it to his right hand.

He hung against the background of smoke like he was pinned there before buckling at the waist, as though his legs were hinged to his body. I'd already rolled over by the time he hit the floorboards with a crash that seemed to shake the house. Fannon had rolled too, trying to disentangle the pistol from the case. He went behind the divan, as quick and as deadly as a poisonous snake.

I put my third shot through the leatherwork about a foot from his ear as he disappeared and I heard him wriggle swiftly away. There was a desk the far side of the room, which commanded a good view of the door. It was a heavy piece which had been made at the turn of the century. Best of all it would provide plenty of cover.

I just made it, Fannon's second slug starring the glass of a bookcase that stood behind it. There was a long silence while the smoke obscured the sunlight spilling in like a pall of fog in a movie depicting Hollywood's idea of London. Incredibly, normal life went on on the far pavement outside the windows; perhaps the house was so solidly built that the uproar couldn't have been heard.

Or the shots had been mistaken for car backfires. Or maybe shots were becoming the normal pattern in Southern California. I couldn't see Fannon now. He was eating carpet somewhere in rear of the divan.

'You're finished,' I said. 'Throw your gun out.'

'Don't be ridiculous, Mr Faraday,' he said calmly. 'We go on to the end.'

'Have it your way,' I said.

I got down in the shadow in rear of the desk and rapidly re-loaded from the spare clip. I had five slugs in there now. And I had all the advantages. Fannon couldn't see me behind the desk and I had the sun at my shoulder. It was true I couldn't see him behind the divan but it was clearly in view and the moment he showed his head I had him.

He must have thought so too because I heard him moving away cautiously a moment or two later. I put another slug through the leatherwork about halfway along the elegant piece, about where I figured his head might have been. More fragments flew around and the slug whined viciously into the far wall, before ricochetting around the room.

Fannon made his break then, running like crazy for the room door, firing over his shoulder. My first slug spun him round before he reached the doorway, the second taking him full in the chest.

I hadn't meant the second because he was already finished, the pistol clattering down; but it was reflexive firing, in the heat of action and I couldn't stop my trigger finger. He sagged, black blood running from his mouth and smirching his immaculate shirt-front. He gave me a last crooked smile and then crashed on to his back. I didn't need to go on over. I knew what I should find.

I got up shakily, re-loaded the Smith-Wesson and put it back in my holster. I went over to the divan and checked out

Fannon's papers. There was a lot of typed stuff in there, mostly business correspondence. Some of it referred to the principal's representative, a Mr Abdullah.

I smiled, looking round at the carnage. It figured. I lit a cigarette, put the match-stick back in the package and feathered out smoke at the ceiling.

I was still sitting there, stitching my frayed nerves together, enjoying the quiet, when a heavy groan broke the silence.

* * *

When I'd climbed down from the bookcase I went over to the thin man. White showed beneath his eyelids. The front of his shirt was a tattered mess. I got my arm behind his shoulders and levered him up, made him as comfortable as I could against the armchair. His eyes flickered and then he was awake.

'I'll get an ambulance,' I said.

He shook his head.

'No good, Mr Faraday.'

His voice was so faint I had difficulty in making out the syllables.

I got my cigarette and put it in a corner of his mouth. He puffed gratefully, the smoke trickling out his nostrils. He looked round the room slowly.

'A shambles,' he breathed. 'It figures.'

His eyes glazed and I thought he was going to pass out. I leaned over him quickly.

'The girl,' I said. 'Myra. You know her address?'

The eyes opened. He was smiling. I took the cigarette out his mouth. The lips were moving. I had to stoop to make out what he was saying.

'Why not? No matter now.'

I took the details down on the back of an old envelope, got him to repeat it. He asked for the cigarette again and I gave it to him. I went over to the far side of the living room to find some brandy. When I came back he was sitting there dead, the cigarette still burning in the corner of his mouth. It was a miracle he'd lasted so long.

I gently removed the stub and crushed it out under my foot before putting it back in the pack. I eased him on to the floor and closed his eyes. I looked round, my legs suddenly feeling shaky. Some set-up. Some gunsel. I walked quickly out and rinsed my head under a tap in the kitchen. I felt better then.

I went around the room for the last time, making sure I'd left nothing behind.

Then I went back out Blue Lagoon the same way I'd come, making sure there was no-one around when I crossed the garage courtyard. Blue Lagoon, Faraday. That was the name of the house. They'd have to call it Red River after this. The film titles were coming thick and fast as I got down in the shelter of the dunes and flogged my way back to where I'd left the Buick in the restaurant parking lot.

I drove back along the coast road, the sting of the sun and the cold rush of the air good on my face, my thoughts rattling around endlessly like billiard balls. Presently I found a small bar on a section of ocean driveway and sat there for an hour or so taking my time over a couple of strong slugs in tall, cool glasses. I'd be a lush by the time the case was over.

The sky was clouding when I left and

tooled the Buick back into the traffic stream and many of the swimmers were leaving the beach.

I checked over my large-scale as I drove, working out the rough position of the address the thin man had given me. I thought I could find it all right. The liquor was beginning to do its work by then but I kept on decelerating and accelerating automatically and changing the gears. I was pretty sober again by the time I hit the edge of town.

17

It was dusk when I got to the girl's place and it was beginning to rain again. I'd checked from a street directory on the way across town and the thin man hadn't lied. He had nothing to lose by telling the truth anyway. She lived in a rented apartment in a fairly ritzy section a mile or two from the Century Plaza.

It was raining nicely by the time I got there and when I'd found somewhere to park I sat in the Buick and smoked a cigarette while I pasted my thoughts together.

That didn't take long and I soon gave it up. I had a good deal of the story but there were still a lot of ends flapping about in there. I'd maybe get those sorted out within the next hour or so. I checked on the Smith-Wesson and put it back in the nylon holster. I didn't think the girl was dangerous; leastways, not to me. She'd done me a lot of good on the case so far but I didn't know who she'd have up there with her.

The directory had just said: M. Dinehart. So maybe Myra Dinehart was her real name. It suited her all right. I wouldn't get any farther forward by sitting around here so I got out the Buick, slammed the door and sprinted down to where some red and white awnings flapped soggily along the façade of a long and very chintzy-looking boutique. I guess someone had forgotten to wind them in when the place packed up on Saturday night.

I had forgotten it was Sunday. The days don't seem to matter at the beach but you always notice it's Sunday in the city when most of the business sections are closed. I gave up the stale philosophy and padded on down beneath the blinds, avoiding the puddles and looking for the apartment court I wanted.

It was the third block down and I was pretty damp by the time I got there. The reception concourse was empty and I studied the apartment numbers which were set out in gold letters on a board fastened to the opposite wall.

I found an empty elevator and rode up to the third floor. There was a mirror screwed to the left-hand teak wall of the elevator cage and I decided I looked pretty frayed around the edges.

I did my best to repair the damage before the cage whined to a halt. I went on down, looking for Apartment 48, the bulk of the Smith-Wesson making a satisfying pressure against my chest. I found it in the end and buttoned the bell-push, waiting in the heavy silence of the corridor where lights burned day and night; a muscle twitching in my cheek, listening to the lonely thumping of my heart.

There was a long delay and then I heard an echoing tinkle from within as though someone had just put a telephone receiver down in a hurry. Maybe the girl had been trying to ring me. I glanced at my watch. It was already a quarter of eight. I'd save her the trouble. Footsteps crossed to the door and then the bolt slid back and it was cautiously opened.

I already had my foot in the opening

and the girl's mouth made a round O of surprise as I gently pushed her back.

'Well, well,' I said. 'Miss Dinehart at last.'

'How did you find me, Mike?' she said in a low voice.

'It's a long story,' I said. 'Aren't you going to ask me in?'

She cast one desperate glance around her as though she felt trapped and then she drew back, motioning me forward into the brightly lit sitting room; the gauze curtains at the long windows giving on to a terrace were drawn back and there was a fine view of the lights of L.A. and the smog.

'Relax,' I said. 'We're friends, aren't we?'

The girl put her hand up to her long blonde hair and patted it absently. It was a purely reflexive gesture and more to give her time to recover her poise than anything else. She led the way reluctantly over to the big stone coloured leather divans that made a U-shape, with the massive brick fireplace on the fourth side. There was a copper jug on the hearth with a big spray of blood-red flowers in it. I'm no horticultural expert but it looked pretty nice.

'I could use a drink,' I said.

The girl flashed me a brief smile.

'Sure, Mike. Scotch all right?'

'Scotch fine,' I said.

Like I said, I'd probably be an alcoholic by the time the case ended but I didn't tell her that. Drink was the only thing keeping me going this week-end.

I sat down on the arm of one of the divans and took a sharp look around the room. There were three more doors leading off. A bedroom, a bathroom and a kitchen maybe. I couldn't hear anything and I guessed she was alone in the apartment. But I wouldn't relax until I'd made sure.

The girl was over at a natural pine buffet the other side of the room now, fooling around with glasses and ice.

'Aren't you going to ask me how I made out?' I said.

She shrugged, putting on a bright face. Her nerves were slowly beginning to come back from the terrace now.

'How did you make out?' she said. 'Was my information correct or not? I was just trying to ring you.'

'I thought I'd save you the trouble,' I said.

She came over and handed me the drink in the long glass. She'd mixed herself some sort of cocktail; whatever it was it looked like it had a lot of powerful stuff in it. We clinked glasses in silence. I relaxed a little, feeling the warmth of the Scotch beginning to permeate my system. It was welcome after the coldness of the rain.

Tonight the girl wore a rust-coloured open-neck shirt that showed off her fine breasts; and dark blue trews that seemed moulded to her figure. She had a brown leather belt with a gold buckle that lay around her waist trimly; her stomach was so flat it didn't need to be tightened. She looked a little white beneath her tan and for the first time I noticed her eyes were a strange violet colour. I suppose it was an off-shade of blue and the lighting in here was doing something to it but it had an odd effect on me.

She hooked over a silver box from the table behind her and took out a Turkish cigarette. I lit it for her and as she put the tip of the cigarette to my match I could see her fingers were trembling. Tonight she wasn't wearing the pearl earrings; just the dress rings on her fingers.

There was a big leather armchair at an angle to the divan and she went over and sat on one arm of that, leaning forward a little, holding her drink in her right hand and the cigarette in her left. She looked pretty uncomfortable to me but I guess she knew what she was doing.

'What happened out there?' she said in a low voice.

I shrugged, taking another pull at my Scotch.

'What you hoped would happen,' I said. 'Fannon and the thin man got dead. That's what you wanted, wasn't it?'

She nodded.

'They were getting dangerous, Mike. Fannon wanted to take over the operation. So he had to go.'

Then a reaction seemed to set in. She didn't quite manage to spill her drink but she came close to it. She stared at me with fright and consternation in her eyes.

'Don't worry,' I said gently. 'They deserved to die. No-one knows what happened yet. The arms are all there, stacked in the garage.'

The girl went on staring at me blankly.

'That's what you wanted to hear too, wasn't it?'

She gulped once or twice like she couldn't get her words out and bit her lip.

'Isn't it time you levelled?' I said.

I leaned forward, fixing her eyes with my own.

'I've killed three men so far on this case,' I said. 'I didn't want to but they would have killed me if I hadn't. I've got to have some answers for the police. And I want some straight answers from you.'

The girl nodded.

'You're right, Mike,' she said dully. 'What do you want to know?'

'You killed old man Frisby, didn't you?' I said.

* * *

There was a long silence in the big room and for the first time I became aware of the faint patter of rain tinkling among the metal tables on the terrace outside and the muffled murmur of traffic from the boulevard far below. Then the girl seemed to crumple; she stared at the floor and I could see her shoulders moving beneath the thin material of the shirt.

'Would you believe me if I said I didn't intend to harm him?'

'You're not a very admirable character in many ways,' I said. 'But you've been square with me. And no, I don't think you're a murderer, if that makes you feel any better.'

The girl looked up then. There were genuine tears. The best actress in the world couldn't have looked like she did then.

'How did you find him?' I said.

Myra Dinehart shrugged, sipping almost fiercely at her drink.

'It was simple, really. That dumbhead Corcoran fouled it up all along the line. I went out to Frisby's apartment. He lived alone, of course, so I knew I couldn't get in there. But I got talking to a neighbour, pretended to be in town for a short time from San Francisco. Sad to miss my uncle when I was just passing through. That sort of thing.'

I grinned.

'I know. It's the same method I use.'

The girl nodded.

'The woman in the next apartment remembered the name of his brother-in-law, said they lived somewhere in Glendale. I checked from the book. It wasn't very difficult.'

'And you got there about an hour before me,' I said.

There was surprise on the girl's face.

'Did I?'

'You must have done,' I said. 'You got in through the open window.'

The girl smiled.

'You're right, Mike. I figured he wouldn't open up if you'd told him to keep a low profile. I felt sorry for him. He was just a frightened old man. But I had to have that information. I was standing between him and the phone. He ran out through the kitchen with me after him and made for the stairs. I guess there was a phone in one of the bedrooms and he wanted to contact you.'

She took a jerky pull at her cigarette before going on.

'I caught him up on the landing. I didn't mean him any harm. But he called me names and slapped my face. I lost my temper then and pushed him. He lost his balance and fell down the stairs. I went after him but he didn't move. His neck was broken. So I got out in a hell of a hurry, the same way I came in.'

I took another nibble at my Scotch.

'You made a fine job of it,' I said. 'I almost got nailed for Frisby's death myself. An old dame turned up and screamed the place down just after I found him.'

The girl smiled briefly, like she'd found something funny in the situation. Maybe there was, come to that.

'We're two of a kind, Mike. Unlucky.'

'Except I'm on the side of the law,' I said. 'I usually come out right.'

The girl swilled the drink around in her glass.

'The game isn't over yet,' she said softly.

'Almost,' I said. 'I only want a few more pieces.'

'Like what?' she said.

'Just exactly what you're looking for,' I said.

She got up from the chair like she'd suddenly remembered something.

'You brought it with you?'

I drew the brown paper envelope from my pocket and tapped it.

'You mean this? I can't make anything of it.'

The girl reached out with trembling fingers.

'Not so fast,' I said. 'I want to hear more.'

I put the envelope back in my inside pocket.

I thought Myra Dinehart was going to cry for a moment.

'You're going to talk, honey,' I said. 'I've been run around long enough.'

The girl bit her lip.

'What is it you want to know?'

'A lot of things,' I said. 'What is that

stuff in the garage at the beach house? Not just pistols and ammunition. That wouldn't call for the floors at Altair to be reinforced.'

Myra Dinehart gave me a tight smile.

'So you've been there?'

I gave her a smile back.

'I haven't been idle.'

I got up then, finishing my drink. I handed her my glass. She put down the Turkish cigarette in a tray on the table, went over to the buffet to refill it. I went round the room while she was doing that, peeked out on to the terrace. The rain was still scything down, making the distant glare of L.A. look faint and insubstantial. I couldn't see signs of anyone else in the place.

There was a jumble of stuff on the left-hand divan, including some of the girl's clothing; there was also a briefcase and a suitcase on the floor.

'Going somewhere?' I said.

The girl came back from the buffet, her eyes flickering nervously from side to side.

'Just out of town for a few days.

When this is over.'

I took the glass from her.

'It isn't over yet,' I said. 'You want the stuff in this envelope. You'll have to work for it.'

The blonde number made a wry mouth.

'I've answered them all so far.'

'You have at that,' I agreed. 'We were talking about those cases.'

The girl bit her lip again. She was getting a lot of practice in.

'It's very sophisticated stuff. I don't know all the ins and outs. Rocket-launchers and guided missile systems, mostly. Destined for the Middle East.'

I stared at her for a long moment.

'You're in a very dangerous business,' I said.

The girl nodded.

'As if I didn't know that. But it's worth big money. This one shipment alone is worth half a million dollars to us. Even split two ways it's worth thinking about.'

I sat down on the arm of the divan again.

'I'll think about it,' I said. 'I still can't

see the problem, Myra.'

The girl shook her head wearily, a cloud of gold hair falling across one eye.

'Your little man,' she said slowly. 'Mr Frisby. He fouled up the works. We always have a fail-safe device with arms shipments. If it's rifles, we remove the bolts and deliver those separately after the balance has been paid. With other weapons it's different components; the stuff is useless without. It's standard practice.'

'So I've heard,' I said, the final pieces starting to click together in my mind.

'Your client,' Myra went on. 'He was just as crooked as anyone else involved. He found the boxes. They were loaded with the firing pins and ancillary mechanisms for the rocket launchers; infra-red sights for other weapons. All of the stuff was useless without them. Frisby removed the boxes and tried to shake down my principal for a share of the action. He was greedy. That couldn't be allowed. So Fannon had to take him out.'

I sat staring at the girl in silence. My face must have told her a lot because she went on, her voice husky and breathless.

'Your little man, Mike. Tired and neglected by the world. That was his only chance to make a killing.'

'Well, well,' I said. 'Now you're telling me something. So he was putting the bite on you for five or ten thousand bucks. But it was a fortune to him.'

The girl shook her head, picking up her glass again.

'He wanted fifty thousand. So he had to go.'

'The bald man tried to take him out and you shifted the stuff,' I said.

The girl nodded.

'We had to stall like mad. Our customer could turn nasty if he knew what the situation was. We've already been paid a deposit, you see.'

'I see,' I said.

I got up and took another turn around the room.

'So your principal's Andrew Grice?' I said. 'Of course. It was his warehouse.'

'Let's leave him out of it,' Myra said quickly.

She got up and came into the middle of

the room, close to where I was standing, lowering her voice.

'Listen, Mike. You have that information on you. It will show where Frisby hid the boxes. It's the key to half a million dollars. And will ensure the continuity of the cash-flow. Like I said we're just a pipeline. The arms will move whether we handle the traffic or not. With Fannon and the others gone there'll be plenty for those remaining.'

'Maybe,' I said. 'I didn't say no, did I?'

The girl put down her glass on the table. She came into my arms then. She was some woman. The kiss seemed to last around ten hours. When I floated back to the floor she stepped gently away from me, holding out her hand.

'Please let me have that stuff, Mike. What's the matter . . . ?'

She frowned, following my glance to the divan where the clothing lay jumbled. I went over and rooted around among the items. The outfit looked familiar. I came up with a black wig, held it high so the girl could see it clearly.

'How's your shorthand speed?' I said.

The girl flushed. She took a little step forward. I could see the cogs of her mind working furiously behind the smooth brow.

'I had to use that disguise to follow you around, Mike. We had to try to keep tabs on you.'

'Sure,' I said. 'The wig and a slightly different makeup had me fooled.'

I took the envelope out my pocket and threw it down at her feet.

'I got the story now,' I said. 'You might as well have this for all the good it will do there.'

The girl was down on her knees, tearing open the envelope when the big man in the dark suit burst through the far door, the barrel of his pistol looking as big as an L.A. freeway tunnel.

18

I was on my knees behind the divan, had the Smith-Wesson out before he was on target. He'd come in too soon, without seeing where we were standing. I shot him through the right shoulder while he was still trying to get his piece to bear. He gave me a look of mingled incredulity and fear. The pistol was already hitting the floor and scarlet spreading on his suit as he sagged against the door lintel and slid down.

The girl gave a little scream, holding the piece of paper and the key in her hand as she stared at the man on the floor.

'He'll live,' I said. 'I only winged him.'

I noticed she didn't go to help him. She was still too busy trying to puzzle out the code I'd cooked up. I went over to the groaning man, kicked the pistol away from his groping hand. I reached in his pocket, got his handkerchief and staunched the wound, propped him against the kitchen doorpost.

'I thought you'd show before long,' I said. 'Only I got the wrong brother.'

'Andrew had nothing to do with it,' he said through his teeth. 'He didn't know what we stored up there.'

'You can tell it to your lawyer,' I said.

'That's the truth,' the girl said.

She came over and stared down at the man on the floor white-faced.

'Frisby tried to blackmail Andrew. He didn't know what the man was talking about. Fortunately, he confided his problem to Howard.'

'Who put Fannon on to him,' I said. 'That's why Andrew Grice was so jittery when I went to see him. Altair must have been a nice cover for you.'

'It was, Mr Faraday,' Howard Grice said.

All the suave geniality had gone from him now. His face looked hard and venial beneath the mask of pain.

'You fooled me all right,' I said. 'But why munitions?'

'I'm an accountant,' Grice said. 'I have

many contacts. A friend asked me to give him storage space some years ago. It grew from that. Latterly, it's been big money. Far more than I could make legitimately. And with very little risk. The stuff is usually passed on within a few days.'

'Save it for later,' I said.

I bent down and put my hand under his shoulder. With the girl helping on the other side we got him on to the divan. The girl went to fetch a shot of something while I picked up Grice's piece and put it in my pocket. There came a knock at the door while I was doing that. I glanced at Grice. His face was white.

'Who's that?' I said.

The girl's lips were trembling.

'A representative of the client come to collect his order,' she said.

She gave me an anguished look. She still held the slip of paper.

'You needn't bother about that,' I said. 'It's gibberish. I made it up myself.'

I grinned.

'I'm in the same boat as yourselves. I haven't any idea where Frisby stashed that stuff.'

I left them there and went over toward the door as the buzzer sounded this time.

'Leave it to me,' I said.

I opened the door on the chain. A tall, slim man with a thin black mustache and an olive skin stood there; an obvious Arab but one of the polished, educated sort.

'Mr Abdullah?' I said.

He gave me a courteous bow.

'Yes. Who are you?'

I poked the Smith-Wesson through the gap.

'The law,' I said. 'The delivery is off.'

He blinked once or twice but his façade didn't crack. He was pretty good come to think of it. He gave me another stiff bow, his brown eyes glittering.

'My advice is to take the next plane out,' I said.

His lips were compressed in a thin line now.

'Tell Mr Grice we will not forget this,' he hissed between his teeth.

'You can take that up with him yourself in due course,' I said.

'We shall do so,' he said again.

'He'll be out in about twenty years,' I told him.

He turned and walked off down the corridor very fast. I stood and watched him until he'd gotten into the elevator. I figured we'd use the rear entrance when we left, just in case he was still hanging around.

* * *

I went back to the two on the divan. There were tears on the girl's face.

'Cheer up,' I said. 'You're young and beautiful. You've plenty of time to make a million.'

'While she's in prison?' Grice said.

His eyes were no longer so blue and so clear above his thick handlebar mustache.

'Who said she's going to prison?' I said.

The girl stared at me incredulously. Even Grice forgot his pain. I went over to the table and picked up my glass to finish off my drink.

'I won't say anything if he doesn't,' I said.

'He's supposed to be your boy-friend, isn't he?'

Grice flushed, like I'd said something indelicate.

'You got it right at last,' the girl said.

'That's very good of you under the circumstances, Mr Faraday,' Grice said.

'I'll say it is,' I told him. 'Especially as you put Fannon on to me.'

I turned to Myra.

'She's been a naughty little girl. But she played square with me. She saved my life. And everything she told me, in her own limited fashion, was the truth. So I'm grateful.'

The girl was staring at me, her lips parted, saying nothing. Like I said, she looked great like that.

'It's only greed spoils her,' I said. 'But time might even take care of that.'

Grice snapped his lips shut. He looked more like his old self.

'Time will certainly take care of me, Mr Faraday. Can't we work out some sort of deal?'

I shook my head.

'There's got to be a patsy. You're the

local Mr Big. You gave the orders. I'm going to find it difficult explaining all those corpses without you. So you get to go down. And it won't be so bad. You'll probably qualify for a state pension by the time you get out.'

'Thanks a lot,' Grice said savagely.

The girl came into my arms. Her mouth was warm and yielding against my cheek.

'I won't forget this, Mike.'

'See that you don't,' I said.

I pushed her gently away. Grice had gotten hold of himself by now. There was a disbelieving look in his eyes.

'I didn't believe they still made people like you, Mr Faraday.'

'They don't,' I said. 'But there are still a few of us left around from the last lot.'

Even Grice forced a smile.

'I'll see Myra's left out of this,' he said.

'Why did you risk appearing in that black wig at the Altair offices?' I said. 'And at Jinty's?'

The girl shook her head.

'It was no risk, Mike. I was following you around, like I said. I just wanted to make sure what you were finding out, where you were going, and that you were following my leads. You didn't recognise me, did you?'

I shook my head.

'There's been enough gabbing for one night. Let's get him out.'

We hauled Grice down the freight elevator in rear of the girl's building without being seen. There was no-one around. I made sure of that. I knew the girl couldn't get Grice away on her own in his condition, even if she tried. I'd gauged her character right. She didn't try.

I brought the Buick back to the alley and helped Grice into the rear seat where he could spread himself. He was in considerable pain now and I broke out my handkerchief and added it to the pad. He passed out while I was doing that.

'You'd best get him to a doctor, Mike,' the girl said anxiously.

I nodded.

'They have good police surgeons downtown,' I said. 'Get on back to your apartment and keep a low profile. With a little luck you won't hear any more of this.'

The girl came up close to the driving window, ignoring the steady onslaught of the rain.

'I'll never forget you for this, Mike,' she said.

'I'll never forget you,' I said.

And meant it. She put her hand up to her hair for the last time.

'We shan't meet again, shall we?'

I shook my head.

'I don't think so,' I said. 'But I'll remember. And don't forget my advice.'

She smiled then.

'I might even take it.'

Her figure dwindled in the rear mirror as I let in the clutch. I had a lot to think about as I drove on over to Central Police H.Q. I stopped at a drug-store on the way. Grice was still out but the bleeding seemed to have stopped. I risked leaving him at the kerbside while I got in a paybooth.

I was lucky. Captain Dan Tucker, an old friend, was on the line. I told him who I was, where and why. He choked once or twice during my long recital but he's a patient man. He said nothing for a moment or two after I'd finished.

'Bring him on down,' he said in the end. 'In the meantime I'll get some people out to that house. You sure you told me everything?'

'I never tell you everything,' I said.

He snorted.

'Your licence comes up for renewal in May,' he reminded me.

'Shouldn't be any problem with your commendations over this job,' I said.

I put the phone down while he was still foaming.

19

It was around midnight when I got to the office. It had been one hell of a case. Tucker had threatened to jug me and throw away the key but that's standard form with him. Grice had been patched up; he'd maybe come out with a stiff shoulder. In addition to his twenty years. I wondered how the girl had gotten mixed up with such a crowd; perhaps she had really once been Grice's secretary and had been slowly drawn in.

Abdullah had taken my advice and gotten the next flight. Tucker had checked with L.A. International. That had been his real name too. There was nothing that could have been done about him anyway as he had diplomatic status. But it served to confirm my story and Tucker had been suitably impressed.

The only snag was Frisby. The police at Glendale had already got the case in hand and I'd rigged the heavy I'd thrown over the cliff for that one. So far as I knew no-one had seen the girl out there and certainly no-one had taken her car number. I understood she'd worn the dark wig when she'd gone there so I guessed she was safe enough.

Grice wasn't talking; he'd promised not to involve her and he hadn't done so. He had no reason to if she was his girl-friend. I felt better then. I'd paid my debt. And it was a big one. I wouldn't be here now if it hadn't been for her.

I went down the corridor and put the key in the door. There was a chair still knocked over in the waiting room where the bald man had outed me. Was it Friday evening? Or a hundred years ago. The side of my face still ached a little as I opened up my inner office door. That was my only souvenir of the case and it would soon fade to nothing.

Frisby certainly hadn't made me rich. I'd been wrong about him from the start. No wonder he'd been afraid; trying to shake down Grice and Fannon and his people was an invitation to suicide. He'd been out to the far edge of fear and gone over. I'd been to the far edge of fear and come back. That was the difference.

I buttoned the office light and went across to my desk. I'd momentarily forgotten what I'd come here for. Then I remembered it was to get my notes on Frisby. There might be one or two points there which could be useful to Tucker in piecing something together to satisfy the brass higher up.

I got the stuff out from under Stella's typewriter and put it down on my blotter. I suddenly felt old and tired and frayed at the edges. I smoothed out the notes and skimmed through them; it was quiet on the boulevard now, save for the occasional shirring of whitewall tyres in the falling rain. The neon made jarring notes of red and green and gold at the window and I switched on my desk lamp to kill the garish shadows.

I jotted down a fresh point or two for Dan Tucker. There was hardly any sound in the office except for the faint scratching of my pen. I thought of Frisby again. Old and tired and frightened; obsessed with his only chance of making a killing in his lifetime; not daring to tell me the truth; and in the end dying by accident as he ran to phone me for help. It figured; it was one of the ironies of the case. Of life for that matter. And all for nothing.

Four people had gotten dead; one wounded, one beaten up; Grice had come out with twenty years if he was lucky; I didn't know about the other brother. He might be in the clear, like the girl said; the police would take care of that. Abdullah's principals had lost their deposit; I hadn't gained a cent and had had my brains half-kicked out. Only the girl had come up smelling of roses.

I was still sitting there when I noticed a small segment of white sticking up from the back of the client's chair; it's a big leather thing with the cushions made to match. Someone had dropped or shoved a piece of paper down the back. I went round the desk quickly, pulled out the fragment.

It turned out to be a sheet of cheap ruled notepaper. I took it over to the desk to read. It was from Frisby; it told what the stuff was and where. He'd spent half a night burying the boxes on waste ground at the rear of Altair's parking lot.

My smile broadened. I was actually laughing by the time I picked up the phone and got through to Dan Tucker.

* * *

The sun was brilliant this morning. I was in by a quarter of nine and made sure the place was in order. I would have had some flowers on Stella's desk if I'd known anything about such things. But I didn't want to let her know how I felt. I sat back at my old broadtop and stared at the cracks in the ceiling. The sun came through the blinds and stencilled heavy grillework patterns on the carpet.

I got up and switched on the plastic fan, which started working to redistribute the tired air. I went back to the desk again and set fire to a cigarette. I put the spent match-stalk in the earthenware tray on my desk. Just then the phone rang. It was Dan Tucker.

He and his boys had spent half the

night digging up the stuff Frisby had buried on the Altair lot. I wondered what Myra would think when she read the newspaper reports and realised how close she'd been to half a million bucks. Or Howard Grice come to that.

I closed my eyes, listening to Dan Tucker's monologue, the sunlight throwing heavy bars of shadow across my eyelids. I told him I'd be downtown again the following morning to cross the ts and dot the is. If you know what I mean. He finished at last and actually thanked me before he put the phone down. I guessed he'd had a commendation from his superiors and was passing some of it on.

I was still sitting there when there came a clitter of high heels from the waiting room and Stella pushed open the office door.

'My, my,' she told the filing cabinet. 'We are a bright and early little man.'

I grinned. Her smile seemed to lighten the whole office and the gold bell of her hair glistened under the overhead lamp. Today she wore a dark red two-piece with a crisp white shirt that dazzled beneath the jacket and her legs in the sheers seemed to go on for ever.

'How was the trip?' I said.

'Just great. But it's good to be back.'

She came over. I had my eyes closed again momentarily. Her lips were warm and soft against my cheek. I felt the sensation all the way down to my socks. She skipped out quickly before I could react. I must have been more frayed-out than I thought.

She carried a black and white striped raincoat like a zebra-skin over one arm and now she put it down together with her brown leather shoulder-bag.

'I brought you a little present.'

'You're spoiling me,' I said. 'What is it? A new truss?'

Stella tried to keep a straight face, couldn't quite manage it. She put the fancy gift-wrapped package on my blotter.

'Just candy,' she said. 'We'll try it out over coffee.'

'I'll drink to that,' I said.

She went on over to the alcove and I heard the snick of the percolator going on. I opened up the package; they were hand-made candies from some famous establishment in New York. I was already salivating when the phone rang again. I picked it up before Stella could get there. It was a woman's voice with something vaguely familiar about it.

'Allday and Allday?'

'Jesus!' I said.

I put the phone down quickly and then left it off the cradle. Stella came back and looked down at me inquiringly.

'What was all that about, Mike?'

'I'll explain later,' I said.

I stubbed out my cigarette in the earthenware tray, listening to Stella clattering around with cups and saucers in back. The pieces of my life were starting to fit themselves together again.

I thought of Myra's face with its cloud of golden hair; Grice's features distorted with pain; Frisby sitting opposite, old and defeated, lying his head off, but coming clean with his piece of paper stuffed down the back of the chair cushion. Extra insurance, perhaps? I would never know now.

The incredulity on the bald man's face as I blew him away; the thin man coming through the door; and Fannon cartwheeling into eternity. It had been a close-run thing as Napoleon said to Josephine. Or one of those Hollywood film characters.

I was back in the present again now. Stella put the coffee cup down on my blotter, went back for her own and the biscuit tin. She looked at me brightly.

'And how were things with you?'

I looked at her steadily. Her presence seemed to fill the whole room.

'Just the usual dull week-end,' I said.

THE END

Books by Basil Copper
in the Linford Mystery Library:

THE HIGH WALL
HARD CONTRACT
STRONG-ARM
SNOW-JOB
A GOOD PLACE TO DIE
THE NARROW CORNER
JET-LAG
TUXEDO PARK
DEAD FILE
BAD SCENE
THE YEAR OF THE DRAGON
DON'T BLEED ON ME
PRESSURE POINT
FEEDBACK
DIE NOW, LIVE LATER
A GREAT YEAR FOR DYING
THE FAR HORIZON
RICOCHET
TRIGGER-MAN
THE EMPTY SILENCE
TIGHT CORNER
SHOCK-WAVE
THE BREAKING POINT
THE HOOK
PRINT-OUT
NIGHT FROST

THE LONELY PLACE
CRACK IN THE SIDEWALK
IMPACT
THE DARK MIRROR
NO LETTERS FROM THE GRAVE
THE MARBLE ORCHARD
A VOICE FROM THE DEAD
A QUIET ROOM IN HELL
HEAVY IRON
DEATH SQUAD
TURN DOWN AN EMPTY GLASS
THE CALIGARI COMPLEX
YOU ONLY DIE ONCE
HOUSE-DICK
SCRATCH ON THE DARK
NO FLOWERS FOR THE GENERAL
THE BIG CHILL
MURDER ONE
THE BIG RIP-OFF
FLIP-SIDE
THE LONG REST
HANG LOOSE
BLOOD ON THE MOON
DARK ENTRY
SHOOT-OUT